"Well, looks like the world ended after all."

Guren recognized the voice.
It belonged to Saito.
To Rígr Stafford. Progenitor of the
second rank.

"Mahiru."

—Yes?

"How much did you know? About what Saito said, about some of his tissue being inside my ancestor's body. Assuming what he said is true, did you already know?"

Mahiru shook her head.

—I didn't know about that. Or should I say even I didn't know about any of that.

It was impossible to trust anything Mahiru said, but it seemed like she was telling the truth this time.

"Even our first encounter was planned."

—*Everything is planned.*

"It was already planned hundreds of years ago."

—*Does that make us soulmates, then?*

"It's not funny."

—*Who's laughing?*

CONTENTS

Seraph of the End

Guren Ichinose: Resurrection at Nineteen

2

Story by Takaya Kagami
Art by Yo Asami

Translated by James Balzer

VERTICAL.

Seraph of the End
Guren Ichinose: Resurrection at Nineteen 2

Editor: Daniel Joseph

Art by Yo Asami.

Originally published in Japanese as
Owari no Serafu - Ichinose Guren, 19-sai no Sekaisaitan 2.

This is a work of fiction.

ISBN: 978-1-949980-14-1

Manufactured in the United States of America

First Edition

Second Printing

Kodansha USA Publishing, LLC
451 Park Avenue South
7th Floor
New York, NY 10016
www.kodansha.us

Seraph of the End

Guren Ichinose: Resurrection at Nineteen

2

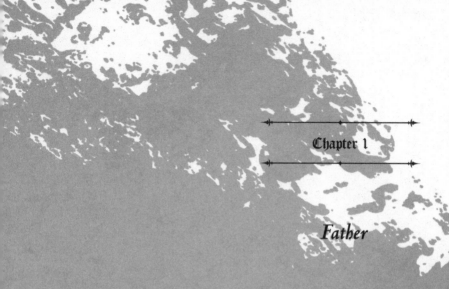

Chapter 1

Father

Seraph of the End

A voice spoke inside Guren's head.

—Shame on you, Guren, you naughty boy. Getting aroused at a time like this.

It was a pretty voice, a girl's voice.
It was Mahiru's voice.
She had used the word "aroused."
Aroused.
But was he really feeling aroused?
He couldn't tell.
With the situation he was in, and the world lying in pieces around him, could he really be feeling aroused?

Guren was running. Racing down the stairs, flight after flight, round and round.
Eighth floor, seventh floor, sixth floor.
"Aroused…? Aroused…"
Sixth floor, fifth floor, fourth floor.
Aroused. What did that even mean? If he had been getting turned on because there was a naked woman standing there in

front of him, then sure, that would make sense. Why wouldn't he be aroused at a time like that?

But that was not the situation he was in right now. He was just running down the stairs, floor after floor.

Running, because a vampire had appeared.

They were in the Meguro ward of Tokyo, near Gakugei University station, along Komazawa Avenue.

An emergency power station was located beneath one of the buildings in the area. At the moment, his friends were working to restart the generators and restore power to the city.

If they could bring the station back online, it would make a world of difference in the lives of the remaining human population.

But they weren't the first to try. Several squads had already been dispatched, and none had returned. Their fates remained unknown.

They had most likely been wiped out by vampires.

The vampire Guren had spotted from his vantage point on one of the upper floors of the building seemed to be sauntering toward the power station, taking his time.

In other words, Guren was about to face off with a vampire.

But vampires were strong.

Extremely strong.

Much too powerful for humans to mess with.

" … "

Guren laid his hand lightly on the sword at his waist.

It was a katana, imbued with demonic power.

Or did it now contain the life force of Mahiru Hiragi?

Either way, the weapon fed on desire. It provided great power, in exchange for the user's humanity.

Vampire or demon.

Which was stronger?

Both were creatures of darkness, but the truth was that vampires were still far more powerful than demons.

And yet Guren was about to fight a vampire.

He might die.

In fact, it was more than likely that he would.

The vampires' power was overwhelming.

So then, why would he be feeling…

"…aroused?" Guren muttered.

Mahiru responded again, inside Guren's head.

—*They say existential drives increase when a person is about to die.*

"So I'm about to die?"

—*Not if I can help it.*

"So I'm just afraid?"

—*There won't even be a fight. Because you're going to speak to this vampire, for Shinya's sake. To save him, and all your friends.*

"Who is this vampire?"

—How should I know? I've never seen him before.

"You want me to have a discussion with a vampire you've never even laid eyes on before?"

—Maybe he's the vampire you need to speak to, or maybe he's just a conduit to someone else. Don't ask me. In fact, he may just happen to be passing by at the wrong time. In which case waltzing up and trying to talk to him would be a terrible idea.

While Mahiru was delivering this coy speech, Guren arrived at the ground floor.

The vampire awaited him just outside.

Vampires had razor-sharp senses. Guren had tried to mask his presence as he ran, but the vampire was probably already aware of him.

And on top of everything else, judging from the vampire's clothing he wasn't just any bloodsucker: he was a member of the nobility. The power of noble vampires dwarfed even that of ordinary vampires.

Guren breathed in slowly.

Then out again, exhaling fully.

He tensed every muscle in his body.

The enemy was strong.

The situation was against Guren.

A single moment's distraction could spell his death.

And if Guren died, Shinya and the others would die too.

Guren had already resurrected them once, wrested them from the grasp of death. But unless Guren did something about it, they would only have ten more years to live.

Which meant that dying right now was not an option. He couldn't afford any mistakes.

"Mahiru," Guren muttered again.

—*Yes?*

"I don't understand the situation. You sure I should approach that vampire?"

—*More or less.*

"That isn't good enough. Shinya's on the top floor—"

—*And ready to shoot. I know.*

"What happens if we kill the vampire?"

—*I dunno.*

"If Shinya sees me talking with him—"

—*It'd be no problem. In and of itself, anyway. But I doubt a vampire will understand your delicate human reservations about Shinya finding out he was resurrected. Of course, if you don't mind Shinya being wiped out of existence…*

"I mind."

—*Then you'd better take care of it.*

"…"

Guren frowned. Sure, that all sounded well and good, but it was because he hadn't been able to "take care of it" that the world had ended in the first place.

Shinya and the others had died.

And all Guren had been able to do was cry. He had been powerless to stop it.

It seemed like Guren was never powerful enough.

Never skilled enough.

But nevertheless…

In, and out—Guren took another deep breath, steeling his resolve.

"Okay. I'll take care of it."

—*Attaboy.*

Guren leapt forward, hurtling through the building's front door and clean over the sidewalk.

Landing in the middle of the road, he spotted the vampire. Its back was turned, and it didn't seem to have noticed him. Or perhaps Guren was such a trivial creature that the vampire saw no point in turning around.

Guren shot a momentary glance upward.

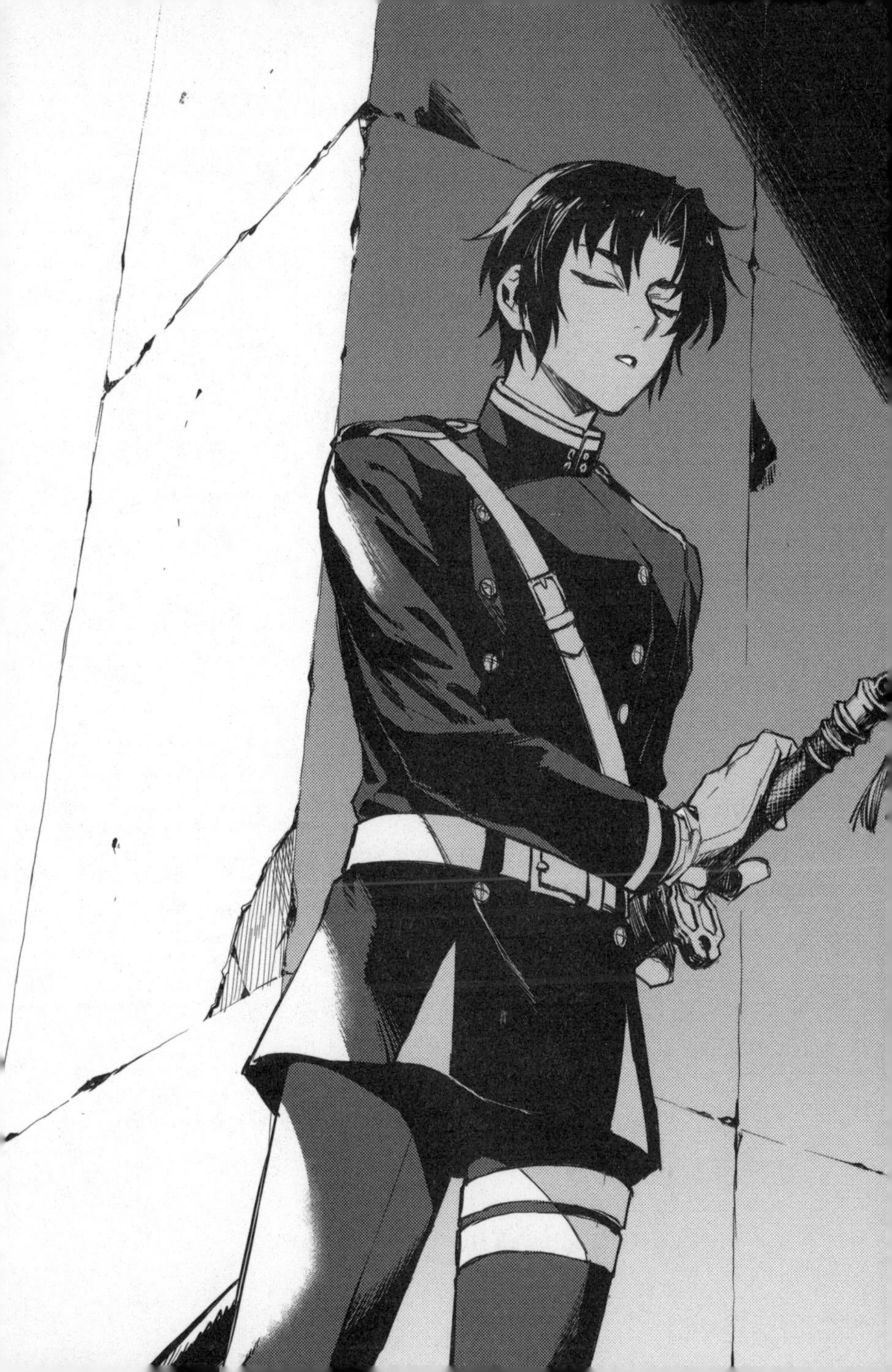

Shinya was probably crouched in one of the top floor windows at this very moment, his rifle trained on the vampire.

Before he had left Shinya's side, they had agreed that Guren would pin the vampire down while Shinya took the kill shot.

Guren placed a hand on the sword he wore at his waist.

—*There it is again, you're so turned on.*

But Guren was pretty sure he didn't feel turned on at all.

—*Then maybe it's just intense bloodlust.*

Now that Guren *was* feeling.

Kill the vampire.

Kill it.

Kill it now.

If he even could, that is.

This vampire was definitely a noble. Guren could tell from his uniform.

He must have noticed Guren by now, but still he didn't turn around.

From a vampire's perspective, a trifling human was no more remarkable than an ant one might step on without even noticing.

Guren slowly drew his sword.

"Mahiru," he said. "It's time."

—*Do it.*

"…!"

Without a word, Guren exploded into the air, closing the distance between himself and the vampire in an instant.

In a split second Guren's blade travelled its course, ready to cleave the vampire's head clean from its shoulders.

However…

"Hm?" the vampire responded languidly, looking back at Guren with no apparent sense of urgency.

Guren had swung his sword as fast as he possibly could, but the vampire was in no rush as he turned to face him, drawing his own sword with an easy grace.

And it was still more than enough time for him to block Guren's blow.

CLANNNNNG!

The harsh screech of metal on metal filled the air.

And Guren finally caught a glimpse of the other's face as their blades crossed.

The vampire had beautiful wavy brown hair, red eyes, alabaster cheeks and red lips, which parted to say: "Hello, human."

The voice was redolent with self-confidence, and a wave of fear swept through Guren.

This vampire was strong—very strong, probably even by the standards of the vampire nobility.

BLAM BLAM BLAM—three gunshots suddenly rang out.

Shinya had fired Byakkomaru.

The vampire's eyes, however, remained fixed on Guren. "Did you think I didn't know he was there? How adorable," he said, reaching toward Guren with his free hand.

"Hrk!"

Guren tried to leap back, but was unable to escape; the vampire grabbed him by the collar, then hoisted him bodily into the air.

"Ahh!" Even as the shout escaped Guren's lips, he could see the white tiger bullets Shinya had fired from Byakkomaru racing towards him.

"Guren?!" he heard Shinya scream.

"Just kidding," the vampire smirked, sounding slightly amused in spite of his apathetic demeanor.

He took one small step to the side, carrying Guren with him.

The white tigers streaked through the space left in their wake and bored into the ground.

The vampire was barely trying.

He could have killed them a thousand times over by now.

Guren's cursed gear should be stronger, now that it contained Mahiru. How was it possible that the noble vampire still held such an advantage?

"No, no, you're very strong," the vampire said, almost as if he could read the despair in Guren's thoughts. "I'd hardly believe you were a human being."

"..."

"Only I'm quite high ranking, even for a noble. Not to mention the fact that my body has been altered."

"Who are you...?"

"I'm a vampire, clearly. A progenitor of the fifth rank."

"..."

Guren had heard that the vampire nobility was divided into ranks.

Supposedly, there were twenty ranks in total, and a vampire's strength increased exponentially the higher it rose.

The fifth rank was very high indeed. Higher even than Ferid Bathory, against whom Guren had been completely helpless.

In other words, if this was an enemy they had to defeat, then the situation was hopeless.

"Shinya! Stay back!" Guren shouted. "He's a fifth-rank progenitor!"

Hopefully Shinya would listen.

The vampire gazed languidly at Guren, still holding him by the collar. He looked to be about twenty-three or twenty-four, but likely he had been alive for hundreds—maybe even thousands—of years.

Guren could glean nothing from the vampire's eyes.

Was he planning to kill Guren? Was he even thinking anything at all?

"So who the hell are you?" asked Guren.

"Are you asking my name, Guren Ichinose?"

The vampire already knew Guren's name.

That meant he *was* the person Mahiru had said Guren needed to speak to.

Which also meant that the things Mahiru was saying to Guren inside his own head weren't just illusions or hallucinations.

That Mahiru herself was not just a hallucination created by Guren's demon.

She lived on inside Guren with a will of her own, and she was still pulling the strings.

Unless...

"..."

...Kureto was right, and Guren was actually the one who had gone on a rampage and killed Shinya, Norito, Mito, Shigure, and Sayuri. He might have been hallucinating this entire time, and created an illusion of Mahiru living inside him as his demon to avoid facing the truth.

Mahiru spoke, interrupting his thoughts.

—Does it matter which is true? Either way, it doesn't change what you have to do.

Don't read my thoughts.

—I wasn't. You were thinking so loudly I could hear every word.

Then from now on I'll close off my mind to you.

—Close it all you want, but that won't change your hopes and dreams. To buy more time for Shinya and the others. To bring me back to life. To bring everyone in the world back to life. In other words, what you really want...

Enough, shut up.

—...*is to be freed from your guilt. That's your one true wish.
Your purpose in life. Your desire. The object of your...arousal.
Come, let's speak with the vampire. What do you think he'll say?*

Guren looked at the vampire. "What's your name?"

"Cæk Sanorium."

"I've never met you before. Or even heard of you. What do
you want with me?"

"It seems my master has taken a shine to you."

"Your master. And who is that?"

"Rígr Stafford."

Guren furrowed his brow. He had never heard of any Rígr
Stafford. Who the hell was—

"I believe you know him as Saito," Sanorium continued.

Now there was a name Guren knew. The man in the suit.

The second-rank progenitor who had assisted Mahiru.

The man who had led her into becoming a vampire.

Guren grabbed Sanorium by the shoulder. "You're after Mahiru, aren't you?"

"Who's Mahiru?"

"Don't play dumb with me."

"I'm not, I assure you. I understand very little of my master's plans. Nothing he does makes much sense to me."

"If you don't understand, then what're you here for?"

Suddenly—

"Guren!"

It was Shinya's voice.

He had come down from his perch and was racing toward

them. Guren glanced in his direction. Shinya had his rifle out and ready.

This was bad.

Sanorium could kill Shinya easily if he wanted to.

And Guren doubted the vampire's orders included keeping Shinya alive.

He had probably been told to contact Guren, and nothing more.

In which case...

"Shinya, it's too late for me. Get back to the power station and—"

Suddenly a strange whirring hum filled the entire surrounding area.

The traffic lights all began blinking.

A thudding, thrumming noise reverberated from the buildings around them, like some great beast coming to life.

"That's strange," remarked Sanorium.

But Guren knew what had happened. Norito and the others had successfully brought the power station back online, and the electric grid was up and running once more.

Which meant that Norito and the others would be coming to rejoin them.

Putting them on a collision course with this monster.

As soon as Shinya realized the power was back on, he froze.

Then he retreated a step, vanishing back inside the building.

Shinya had pulled back immediately. He knew he couldn't save Guren on his own.

But once the others arrived, they would probably attack en

masse.

Guren had to wrap up his conversation with Sanorium before that happened. "There isn't much time. If you have something to say to me, say it quick."

"Me? What would I possibly have to say to you?"

"Then, why are you here?"

"I honestly don't know. I'm just supposed to give you a good toss, so that your friends don't think you've betrayed them. Oh, and don't worry. I was ordered not to kill them. Though I might drink a little of their blood."

Sanorium was still holding Guren by the collar and, evidently finished speaking, he swung his arm in a rough arc, hurling Guren away with all his considerable might.

Guren careened through the air at breakneck speed, but even as he rocketed away, he caught sight of his five friends assembling to face Sanorium.

Shinya, Norito, Mito, Shigure, Sayuri.

Even the five of them together were no match for their opponent. At best, the vampire would merely toy with them. The disparity in strength was just too great.

Shinya was turned toward him, and Guren saw a look of relief cross his face when he realized that his friend was still alive and had been removed from the battlefield.

Guren felt a sudden impact against his back as he collided with the wall of a building and broke his spine. His internal organs turned to jelly.

He went clean through the wall and landed on the ground inside the building.

"Ngh… Urk…"

The damage he had suffered was devastating.

The demon's curse kicked in quickly and his injuries began to heal, but it would take some time before he could move again. With his back broken, he couldn't even stand up.

A voice came from somewhere above his head.

"Well, looks like the world ended after all."

Guren recognized the voice.

It belonged to Saito.

To Rígr Stafford. Progenitor of the second rank.

But Guren couldn't move his body. He couldn't move his neck, couldn't turn to look in Saito's directi—

Just then, the bones in his spine finished knitting themselves back together, the nerves reconnected, and he was able to lift his head again. He managed to sit up.

"Ngh…" Guren groaned, dragging himself into a seated position.

Sure enough, standing before him was a pale, dark-haired man wearing an expertly tailored suit.

His eyes, however, were black—he lacked the characteristic red eyes of other vampires.

"What's the point in wearing contacts now?" asked Guren, staring into those black eyes.

"It makes me seem more human."

"But you're not human."

"Nor am I vampire, though, not anymore."

"Then what the hell are you?"

"That's an interesting question. Do any of us really know

what we are? Do you?"

Guren thought for a moment. "I'm human."

"Well, that much is true. You're clearly not a dog or a cat, anyway."

" … "

"But vampires were human once as well, you know. Just as Mahiru Hiragi was."

"*You* turned her into a vampire."

"But she isn't a vampire anymore, either."

Guren gripped the handle of his sword. Mahiru had devoured a demon and now resided inside him. He had no idea *what* she was at this point.

Or even whether she was alive or dead.

"What did you do to Mahiru?" Guren demanded.

"Exactly what she wanted."

"She swallowed a demon and went inside me."

"Yes, I know."

He knew?

Then, he must know what had happened to her.

Guren stood and levelled his sword—the sword containing Mahiru—at Saito's throat.

Saito looked down, casting his black eyes along the length of the blade. "Hmm."

"What the hell did you do to her?"

"I told you, I did exactly what she wanted."

"And what was that?"

"For you to survive."

"She… What…?"

"She wanted to become your strength, to support you from within."

"And you helped her do that?"

"Well, I wouldn't want to take all the credit. Certainly I helped with some of it, but who's to say?" Saito replied, slowly pushing Guren's blade out of the way with one hand before continuing. "Tell me something, Guren. What do you think of this world?"

Guren wasn't sure he understood the question.

Was Saito asking Guren's opinion of the world, now that it had been destroyed? Or was he asking what Guren thought of the world in general, a place where one had to go on living even though nothing ever went the way it was supposed to?

Saito went on. "Who do you suppose built this world? Who made it the way it is?"

Apparently he had meant the latter.

Why were things the way they were?

"How should I know?" retorted Guren. "Go read some philosophy."

"Philosophy? Ha, nonsense written by people whose lifespans measure only the tiniest fraction of my own."

"If it's how long he's been alive that makes a person wise, then you're barking up the wrong tree... I'm only sixteen, remember?"

"Hahaha, good point. Though for a boy of only sixteen, you've certainly been through a lot," chuckled Saito.

Guren turned, and gazed out through the hole his body had made in the wall of the building. The world on the other side lay in ruin. All of the adults were dead.

"You're telling me…" he muttered.

Saito continued. "I went through something similar, you know. I was maybe about the same age you are now when it happened."

"It? What do you mean 'it,' what happened?"

"Perhaps I should say when *he* happened. I was sixteen at the time, maybe seventeen. Or was I already in my twenties at that point? It was so very long ago, my memory's grown hazy."

"And? What are you talking about?"

"I'm talking about the only man in this world who's been alive longer than I have."

"You mean…"

"The man who turned me into a vampire. The first vampire. The first progenitor. The Sire."

Guren stared at Saito. He still had no idea what Saito was getting at.

It was the stuff of myth, something that had happened thousands of years ago.

"What's your point?" asked Guren.

Saito held up a finger, and went on. "I believe the story of this world has by and large been written by that very man."

Guren didn't understand what Saito meant, but Saito continued anyway.

"Who lives where? What power is bestowed on whom? What religions rise up in which regions? The fate of nations, who is given to sorcery and magic—the Sire's influence can be seen in all of these things. What, where, and how—he directs it all to some degree."

"What is he, a god?" asked Guren.

"More or less," answered Saito with a laugh. "But he isn't a god, not really. He's a vampire."

"And?"

"And I've been pursuing him."

"Why?"

"That's for me to know."

"Huh?"

"Even if I told you, you wouldn't understand. You haven't lived long enough to comprehend it."

"Then what does any of this have to do with m—"

Saito cut him off. "You are not a scion of his tale. You are *my* child."

"..."

What was *that* supposed to mean?

Saito's child?

"My father's already dead. His name was Sakae Ichinose."

"That is entirely beside the point."

"Then what is the point?"

"Hmm, let's see, where should I begin? Ah, I know. There are two separate occasions on which I've played a significant role in shaping the history of magical society in Japan. Though I imagine you already know about one of them."

To be honest, Guren wasn't sure what Saito was talking about, but that didn't seem to be a problem. Saito was very talkative today. And Guren knew from experience that Saito couldn't be trusted when he got talkative.

Nevertheless, Guren remained silent and listened.

"The first," Saito went on, "was when I created the Brotherhood of a Thousand Nights. I did so in order to oppose the Order of the Imperial Demons."

"So that means that the Imperial Demons were created by this 'Sire' you're after?"

"Yes, very perceptive," replied Saito, smiling. "Though when it comes to it, nearly everything in this world is his creation."

His creation?

Saito's choice of words sounded oddly religious. Was the Sire really that powerful?

Like a god after all.

"Things didn't go according to plan, however," continued Saito. "Although I was the one who created the Thousand Nights, they never seemed to do what I wanted them to. They began conducting their own research without my knowledge. Research, in fact, that seemed to play right into the Sire's hands. It almost seemed like my creation of the Brotherhood had been part of his plan all along. What was I to do? The more I tried to catch up with him, the farther ahead he seemed to get. I felt like Sun Wukong trapped atop Buddha's palm."

Funny. The story of Buddha and the Monkey King was old, but Saito was even older.

"So I took a different tack. I would do nothing. Instead, I would change what he was doing. I planted my own seeds in the fields the Sire had plowed."

"So what did you change?"

Saito raised two fingers this time.

"This was my second major act within the magic-using world. Hundreds of years ago, I arranged for the second most powerful and influential clan in the Order of the Imperial Demons after the Hiragis—the Ichinose Clan—to come into conflict with their masters."

Guren felt his pulse quicken.

The event Saito was referring to had changed the course of destiny for the entire Ichinose Clan. The fallout from it had tormented them ever since. The Ichinose Clan had once been the most prosperous of houses. Now they were the most despised, regarded as traitors.

Ever since that time the Ichinoses had languished upon the lowest rungs of magical society, crushed beneath the bootheels of the other houses.

Guren's own father had been laughed at, disparaged, and still he had bowed to his own execution.

All who were born into the Ichinose Clan carried this curse from the moment of their birth.

Traitors. Scum.

Filthy, lowborn vermin.

Saito went on. "I used a woman to do it. She was an alluring girl. With a little extra help from my sorcery, she drove a wedge between the clans in no time at all. The Ichinoses became pariahs, the clan itself teetering on the verge of dissolution. But there too I intervened. You see, this story, it's not like the movies. There's no happy ending waiting at the end of all the heartbreak. The heroine in our story was raped by the Hiragis, she conceived a child, and into that child I inserted a small amount of tissue from my own body. So you see, if you're descended from that child…"

Guren suddenly swung his sword.

With all his strength, with intent to kill.

Maybe Saito was telling the truth. Maybe he was lying. Guren no longer cared.

This was all a joke to Saito. Did he have any idea what life had been like for the Ichinose Clan over the centuries? What they had gone through? None of it mattered to Saito, he was laughing about it all.

So Guren swung at him.

But Saito easily intercepted the blade with his two raised fingers.

Guren pushed harder, using all his strength. And if his own strength wasn't enough, he would call on the demon's strength, on every last drop of power from the demon's curse.

Dark magic coursed over Guren's arms, up his shoulders to his neck, his face.

"I'll kill you!" roared Guren, but his sword didn't budge.

"Look at how strong you've become," said Saito, still smiling at him. "You make daddy so proud."

"You're not my father!"

"True, I'm more like your great-great-great-great-great-great-grandfather. Which makes us practically strangers, I suppose."

Guren pulled back his sword and swung again.

Saito merely tilted his head to the side and dodged the blow.

But Guren was undeterred.

"Die!"

"Haha."

"Die!!"

"Hahaha."

"Die!!!"

"Hahahaha."

Saito's laughter echoed in Guren's ears, drowning out all other sounds. Guren still wasn't strong enough to beat him, not even close.

Saito raised a hand lightly into the air, and then brought it down sharply, slapping Guren across the face. The force nearly took his head off, and his body slammed to the ground.

Guren's neck was definitely broken. He couldn't breathe. His head swam, his mind unable to form a coherent thought.

Saito went on. "No human being could survive a blow like that. It really is impressive how powerful you've become."

"..."

"Let me tell you something, Guren Ichinose. The Sire has no interest in the human heart. What you think about, how you live, who you love or hate—it's all meaningless to him."

"..."

"Perhaps it's because he's too complete, too immaculate. Or perhaps it's just that he's lived too long. But he disdains the human race."

"..."

"It was no different when the Ichinose Clan was cast out for the sake of love. He let it happen. It didn't strike him as important. He had never considered how much power there could be in love, or jealousy, or anger. And as a result the Ichinoses were expelled. This split made way for the rise of the Brotherhood of a Thousand Nights."

"..."

"Then again, who knows, maybe this was all part of his plan too. Maybe I really am Sun Wukong after all, tiny and helpless in the palm of the Sire's hand. Who's to say?"

The bones in Guren's neck finally knit themselves back together, and he lifted his head. "What could you possibly hope to achieve with me?"

Saito looked down at Guren with an almost tender look. "You are my scion. I made you to resist him. To abduct the maiden from the pages of his story."

The maiden.

Guren knew immediately who Saito was referring to.

It was a chance encounter that should never have happened.

How were Guren and the Hiragi girl able to meet, down by the banks of the river on that fateful day?

And why had Mahiru and Guren fallen in love so quickly, so easily—?

"So my...our...feelings for each other—"

Saito cut him off. "—Had nothing to do with me. I just brought you two together, and the wheels of fate turned on their own. You fell in love. Almost as if it was a foregone conclusion."

"..."

"I sincerely hope that it was God's hand at work, and not the Sire's. Or, if not God's…"

Saito trailed off.

"What?" asked Guren, but Saito smiled and didn't answer. Instead, he produced something from his breast pocket.

Guren couldn't tell what it was, but it was small, and looked like a crucifix.

Or, a dagger?

"What is that?" he asked. Still no response.

Mahiru, however, materialized next to Saito. He didn't seem to be able to see her, but apparently he didn't need to.

"I sense a presence," Saito said. "Are you here?"

—Even if I say yes, I doubt you'll be able to hear me.

She was right, it didn't seem as if her words had reached Saito.

"She's standing next to you," Guren told him.

"That's what I thought."

"What's that dagger for?"

"That's for me to know."

"Mahiru."

—Yeah?

"Do you know?"

—No.

Just then, Saito brandished the dagger above his head and brought it down.

A moment later, it pierced Mahiru's throat.

Mahiru had no body. Saito couldn't even see her. And yet there the dagger stood.

—*Ah!*

A short cry escaped Mahiru's lips.

She put her hands to her throat and collapsed to the ground.

"What did you do?!" Guren screamed, but Saito seemed unconcerned.

"Nothing much," he replied. "I just hid something."

"What?"

"A sin."

"Whose sin?"

"You'll find out soon enough. We're going to need to collect these sins, if our wishes are to be granted. Now then, my work here is done. It's about time I departed. Loiter here too long and the Sire is bound to find me."

"Wait! Aren't you going to explain—"

"You'll reach me whether I explain or not. After all, I made you to serve me. You're my children."

"Don't give me that—"

But just then, Shinya crashed through the wall and tumbled into the room.

"Gah, grk," a spray of blood erupted from his lips. Appar-

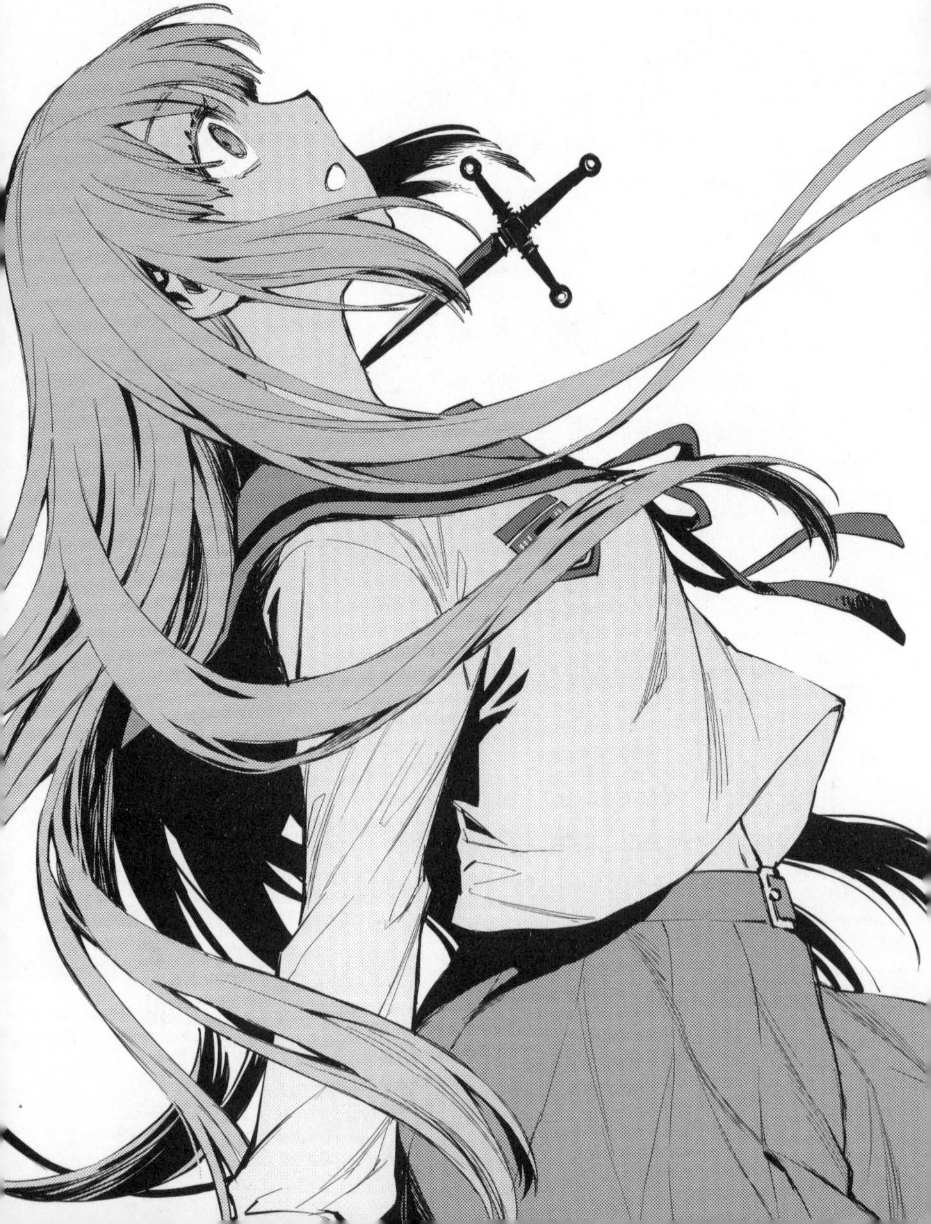

ently the fight with the noble vampire who called himself Sanorium raged on outside.

Shinya caught sight of Guren, and asked, "Guren! Are you
hurt?"

Guren turned to look at Saito before answering.

But he was nowhere to be seen.

He had vanished.

Mahiru turned towards Guren.

—He's gone. But I'm sure we'll see him again.

She crouched down then, her skirt riding up just enough to
expose her slender, attractive knees.

Guren followed her gaze to where something that looked
like an envelope lay on the ground. What was inside? A letter?
Something else?

—Don't look at me. Shinya will catch on.

"..."

*—Saito dropped it there before he left. Try and pick it up with-
out Shinya noticing, and then we can rejoin the battle with the
noble.*

"Guren, are you alright?" Shinya broke in.

"Huh? Uh huh. I mean, no. I broke my neck."

"Damn."

"It's almost healed, though. How's it going out there?"

"Badly," answered Shinya, fixing his eyes on the hole his body had made in the wall. "That vampire's too strong. We haven't even made a dent."

"So what happens now?"

"I don't know, but I don't think he's planning to kill us. I hate to admit it, but I think he's been holding back. He could kill us if he wanted to."

But he wasn't going to.

The reason was simple. He had just been waiting for Saito to finish his conversation with Guren.

Or was it a conversation with Mahiru?

Guren touched his neck gingerly as he peered outside, acting as if he were still nursing the break. He took a few steps back.

Just far enough to put his foot over the envelope Saito had left on the ground.

Shinya had never noticed it.

"What's the vampire after?" Guren wondered aloud.

"Who knows? Our blood, I imagine."

"Has anyone been bitten?"

"Not yet. But it's just a matter of time. There must be some way we can defeat him."

Guren wasn't even sure if defeating Sanorium would be a good idea or not.

He returned his sword to its sheath and crouched down, shrinking into himself like a tightly wound spring.

"Getting ready to jump back into the fray?" asked Shinya.

Not quite. Guren had a different reason for adopting that

pose.

While Shinya was speaking, Guren had already transferred the envelope beneath his foot to the palm of his hand, then slipped it into his breast pocket. He didn't have the faintest clue what might be written inside, but it seemed there was still a ray of hope left in their story after all.

Greater forces were at work.

Wheels were turning that could lead to superior magic.

And if one of those wheels just so happened to be Guren, there might still be a future for them.

Maybe Guren could even use the situation to his advantage, to permanently resurrect Shinya, Norito, Mito, Shigure, and Sayuri.

If there was a power out there even greater than the one that had destroyed the world, then it might not be too late to shine some small light on the darkness of his despair.

Hope. They still had hope.

"Shinya," Guren said.

"Yeah?"

"I'm going to take it to the limit, go full rampage. You do the same. We'll hit him fast and hard."

"And if that's not enough?"

"Then we get the others and run like hell."

"Think we'll be able to get away?"

"If our opponent isn't serious about killing us, I think we'll be alright. If we run as fast as we can he might not even chase us."

"That's not much of a strategy."

"Do you really think strategy is going to work on an opponent that strong?"

"Not at all."

"Exactly. In the end, we humans are still weak. We need to get much, much stronger."

"If we get any stronger than this, I'm not sure we'll be human anymore."

But Guren wasn't so sure that a body that could completely heal itself after a broken neck and back could still be called human anyway.

Never mind Shinya and the others, who'd come back from the dead thanks to forbidden magics.

Could any of them still be called human?

Or were they something else entirely?

It didn't matter.

So long as they could survive this, they might still have a future.

"We go on the count of three. Ready?"

"Ready. One—"

"Who said you get to count?"

"Two."

Guren narrowed his eyes, willing the dark magic to course through his body.

He would need it all.

Every last bit.

Every drop of desire he could possibly feed to Mahiru.

—Most of your desires taste of guilt, Guren.

Mahiru sounded disgusted, but Guren ignored her.

"Three."

As the word was leaving Shinya's lips, Guren released all the potential energy coiled in the tightly wound spring of his body.

"AHHHHHHHHHHHHHHHHHHHH!"

He burst through the hole in the wall, rocketing clear across the sidewalk and into the street.

To the place where even now his friends were locked in battle with the vampire.

Or should have been—

"…"

There was no longer any battle being fought there.

Norito, Mito, Shigure, and Sayuri lay sprawled in the street.

But Guren realized immediately that they were still alive. The dark magic running through his veins had drastically heightened his senses, and he could feel them breathing. He could sense their heartbeats.

"G-Guren," groaned Mito, noticing him first.

On hearing her voice, Guren's two retainers, Sayuri and Shigure, looked his way as well.

"Ah, ah!"

"Master Guren, you're alright."

He was, but his friends didn't seem to be.

Norito was the last to turn his head in Guren's direction.

"Where's the enemy?" Guren asked him.

"He bailed," Norito replied.

"So why are you lying on the ground?"

43

"I'm just so tired."

"Huh?"

"He drank so much of my blood, I feel wiped out. He drank from all of us."

Guren scowled.

He had been drained by a vampire not so long ago himself. The man named Ferid Bathory had forced him to give up his blood to save his friends.

Guren recalled how it had felt.

The overwhelming ecstasy that accompanied the sensation of his lifeforce being extracted from him before his very eyes. The terrible humiliation of finding pleasure in the liberation brought by death.

"…"

Guren looked down at his friends where they lay on the ground.

Mito, Shigure, and Sayuri's tired faces were slightly flushed.

Mito covered her face with her hands and said, "Please don't look at me, Guren."

Guren understood. He had felt the same way after Ferid had drained his blood.

He averted his eyes.

Shinya approached from behind, repeating Guren's question.

"Where's the vampire?"

"Apparently he left once he was full."

"Where'd he go?"

"Who knows?"

"Guess we got lucky."

Guren scanned their surroundings.

The streets were deserted.

Cars lay toppled over on their sides.

Buildings had been reduced to rubble by falling airplanes.

The world lay in ruins. Could they really call themselves lucky?

"Well, we're still alive, so lucky enough, I guess," Guren replied. "Plus, the power's back on. Good job, you guys."

Guren turned back toward his friends, who were already staggering to their feet.

Shigure and Sayuri's faces lit up at Guren's words of praise.

"Did you hear that, Yuki?" asked Sayuri. "Master Guren said we did a good job."

Shigure nodded, evidently pleased as well.

Mito looked up at the blinking traffic light overhead. "Maybe things will start to get a little better now that the power is back on."

"At the very least," put in Norito, staring at the others with the utmost seriousness, "once it gets dark, we'll finally be able to watch some real hardcore porn aga—ow yow yow!"

Mito had just punched him square in the face.

Well, he had it coming.

Ignoring them, Guren sheathed his sword.

He stretched, and gave a little sigh before speaking. "I'm starving. Let's go home."

"Yes, sir!" shouted Sayuri and Shigure.

Their mission was over.

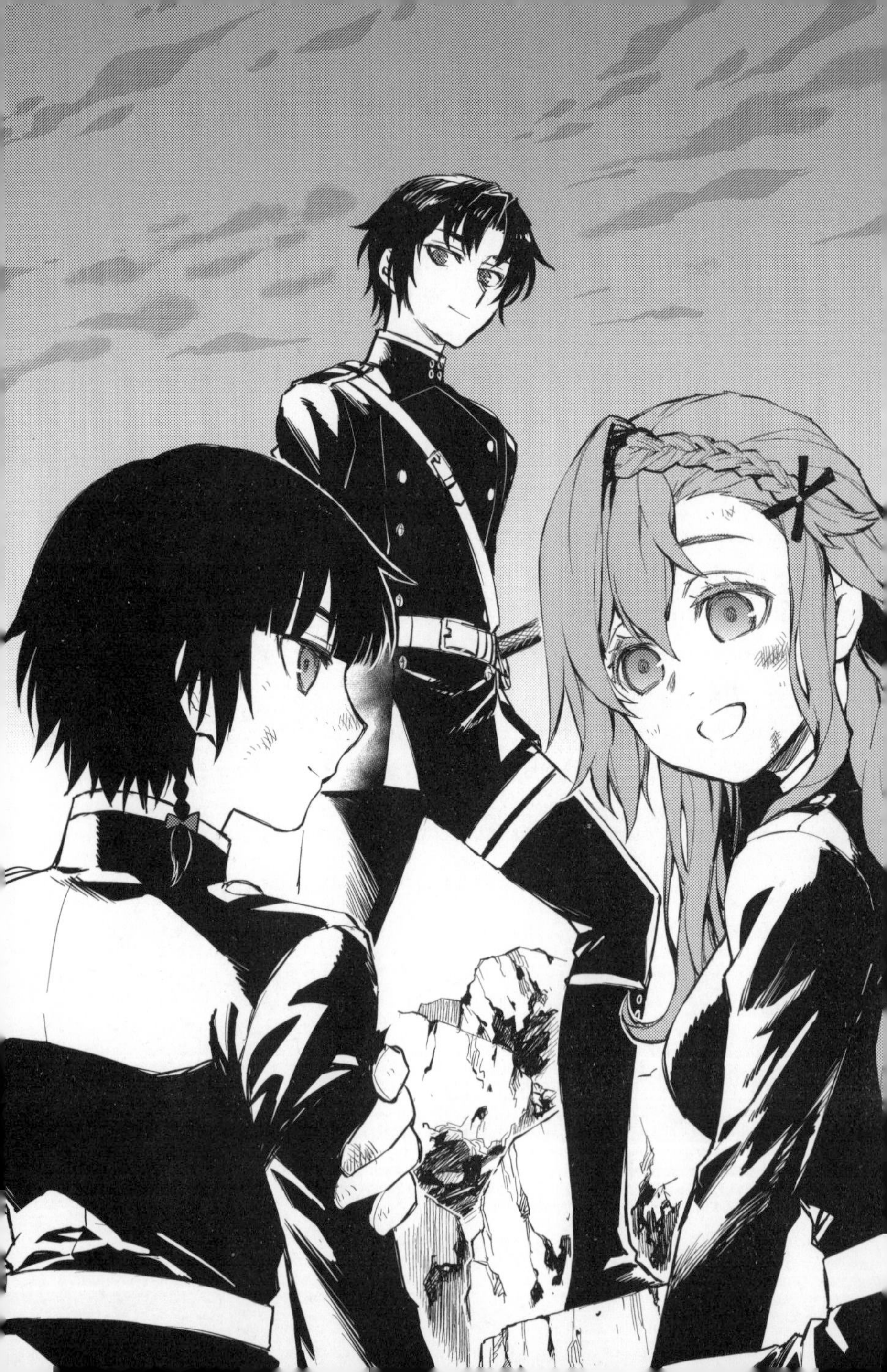

For now, at least, the power was restored.

The group began preparing to head back.

They laughed and joked with each other, the tension finally starting to fade.

"…"

As Guren watched them, he slowly reached into his jacket.

For the envelope in his inside pocket.

He drew it out carefully, so the others wouldn't see.

—*Are you really going to read it right now?*

Guren ignored Mahiru and opened the envelope.

—*I'm feeding on your desire to know the secret even as we speak, Guren.*

There was a document inside the envelope. Guren took it out and unfolded it.

—*I love you, Guren. I'm so happy that I get to be here inside you.*

Guren scanned the paper.

It contained information on two test subjects.

It gave their location, when they could be rescued, even the best way to go about it.

The names of the two test subjects Guren was meant to

rescue were listed there as well:

Yuichiro Amane
Mikaela Shindo

Guren stared at the two names on the page, his lips moving silently.

"Who the hell are they?"

Chapter 2

*The Boy Who Wished
the World Would End*

Seraph of the End

Far, far, far away.

The Earth's surface was so far away.

A deafening whir filled the air—the sound of spinning helicopter blades. Mingled with the noise of the blades was the softer sound of children sniffling and crying.

"What's happening?"

"Th-The Director… She's… She's…"

Yuichiro stared at the sobbing children. One of the younger girls clung to his chest.

"I'm scared, Unky Yu…"

The girl was shaking. Yu didn't know her name. He had only just arrived at the orphanage, after all.

And it had happened so soon after he got there.

The woman in charge of the orphanage, who called herself the Director, had died, blood suddenly spouting from her nose, mouth, and eyes.

And then pandemonium had erupted.

Tongues of flame sprouted all across town, and screaming voices filled the air.

The children had waited helplessly in the orphanage, but then the windows shattered and monsters came pouring in.

Guren Ichinose: Resurrection at Nineteen

Monsters with crimson eyes and sharp fangs.

They laughed as they began to drink the children's blood.

There was no resisting them.

Crying and screaming availed the children nothing.

They could but submit to this monstrous feeding frenzy.

And as their blood was being drained from their bodies, a booming voice reached them from outside:

"Attention! The foolish humans have released a deadly virus! Regrettably, the human race has fallen! However, it appears as if children under the age of thirteen have not been affected..."

The voice was saying that the world had ended.

Hearing that, however, didn't make Yu feel much of anything. For him, the world had ended long ago.

When his father had denounced him as a demon child and tried to kill him.

When his mother, tortured by the guilt of having birthed such a monster, had tried to commit suicide by lighting herself on fire.

These were Yu's only memories of the world.

All he could recall was his parents screaming at him, calling him a monster.

With no other memories to fall back on, Yu didn't have a strong reaction to the sudden news that the world had ended.

So what, who cared?

There was nothing in this world he would miss.

Yu had always been alone.

Life had no meaning, no value. He was on his own.

"Unky Yu," came another voice.

More children were now huddled around him. He didn't know any of their names, either. They huddled against his chest, their faces smeared with tears.

Yu felt flustered by the warmth radiating from their little bodies.

"..."

He—they—were inside a helicopter the vampires had brought.

Yu had no idea where they were being taken.

For that matter, he wasn't even sure where the orphanage had been located. He was pretty sure it had been called the Hyakuya Orphanage, though.

His only other memories were of being kept in a cell.

And of a strange girl coming to speak with him.

And of being brought to the orphanage by a man in a black suit, named Saito or something.

Other than that, he remembered almost nothing.

That didn't seem strange to him, however.

He knew that he had been put in that cell because he was worthless and his parents reviled him.

He knew that there was no place for him in this world, no value to his existence.

And yet...

"..."

...these other children were suddenly clinging to him. It made his head spin.

Yu looked up and saw a boy and girl closer to his own age sitting across from him.

The boy, who was apparently named Mikaela, was the same age as Yu. The other children at the orphanage seemed to gravitate toward him, and when Yu had arrived, Mikaela had held out his hand and said they were going to be family. Family? Who said that to someone the first time they were introduced?

The girl was named Akane. She was a year younger. She still seemed a little wary of Yu. Which made sense, they had only just met. Besides, she'd find out soon enough.

That Yu was a devil child, that he wasn't worthy of her friendship. After all, that's what his parents had said, so it had to be true. It had to be. It's what everybody had said.

But the girl named Akane, her cheeks stained with tears, herself hugging several small children to her chest, looked back at him and said, "Thank you, Yu."

"Me? For what?"

"For holding the children like that."

"I didn't do anything, they all came to me."

"Kosuke and Yumi get scared easily, and they're not good with new people, but they're coping with all this thanks to you, Yu. If... If it weren't for you..."

She didn't have to finish her sentence, Yu knew what she was going to say.

They had all seen what would've happened to Kosuke and Yumi if they were bawling and making a scene.

There had been other kids in the helicopter with them, children who weren't from Hyakuya Orphanage. But some of them had been crying and screaming, and to shut them up the vampires had thrown several of them out of the helicopter by way of example.

It had worked.

But really, it was Yu, Mika, and Akane, holding them close and whispering that everything would be alright, that was keeping the children quiet.

Don't cry, everything's alright.

Don't be scared, everything's alright.

We'll protect you, everything's alright.

Everything's going to be alright, so don't cry, don't cry.

"..."

Of course, they all knew that it wasn't alright.

The adults were all dead.

The world lay in ruins.

And they had just been kidnapped by vampires.

It was pretty clear that nothing was going to be alright.

But the three of them just kept whispering, *it's alright, it's alright, it's alright*, over and over again.

"I-If you two weren't here," Akane began again, "I don't know what...what I would..."

"Come on, don't cry, dummy," said Yu. "Everything's gonna be alright."

Akane stared at him.

"Yu's right," Mika chimed in from where he sat beside Akane. He turned to look at her. "We're family. As long as we're together, everything will be alright."

"Y-Yeah, you're right," said Akane, her face contorting with emotion. "Everything's gonna be alright."

They all fell silent. But they continued to bite their lips and cry under their breath. Their shoulders shook with silent, hiccupping sobs.

Eventually, Akane and the younger children fell asleep.

Yu looked around at their faces, and realized that Mika was staring at him.

"…"

"…"

Mika's eyes remained fixed on Yu's face.

"…"

"…"

Yu scowled. "What?"

"Nothing."

"Then stop staring at me!"

"I'm not staring."

"Well you're looking at me."

"Where else am I supposed to look?"

"Anywhere."

"Such as?"

"Look at the vampires."

"They're terrifying."

"Then look at the ceiling."

"There's nothing to see up there."

"There's nothing to see here, either. You trying to pick a fight?"

Mika shrugged, a mischievous expression on his face. "Why yes, of course I am. Come on over here so I can knock you out," he joked, his arms piled high with sleeping children.

Yu sighed in exasperation. Then he breathed in again,
"Haah…" and let out another, deeper sigh.

Mika laughed. "Come on, it's not that bad."

"No? Look around you," Yu retorted, taking in their situation.

They were in a helicopter piloted by vampires, headed towards God knows where.

The world had been destroyed.

And a bunch of children he had only met earlier that day were sleeping huddled against his chest.

"Who are these kids, anyway," Yu asked, looking down at them.

"They're your family," Mika answered.

"I ain't got a family."

"You do now."

"Get real."

"I am being real."

"Seriously, get real!"

"Who else have you got? Weren't you telling me that your parents called you a demon, that they abandoned you?"

Mika's words recalled the scene to Yu's mind. The fear on his parents' faces, when they tried to kill him.

"You don't know a fucking thing about me," Yu shot back, glaring at Mika.

But Mika just smiled. "I told you, we're the same."

"The same how?"

"My parents tossed me out of a moving car."

"..."

"I'm pretty sure they got rid of me because they just didn't want me."

"..."

"All the kids at the orphanage were abandoned. Take Akane. Apparently she was abandoned because she freaked out and used a kitchen knife to stab one of the naked grown-ups who was chasing her around."

"..."

"And Kosuke and Yumi ended up at the orphanage because—"

"Who cares? Just because we all got a raw deal doesn't make us family," Yu spat out angrily.

But Mika just kept on smiling. "Then what does make someone family?"

"..."

"The people who tried to kill you, were they family?"

"..."

"The people who tried to kill me?"

"..."

"Maybe those people who were chasing Akane around?"

"..."

"Or maybe you think that none of us deserve to have families? Well try telling that to those kids sleeping on your chest right now," Mika finished.

Yu frowned, looking back down at the children in his lap. Despite the desperate circumstances, despite all the screaming and tears, the children's sleeping faces were so innocent and contented.

Their expressions were so totally peaceful.

And they were warm.

"..."

So terribly warm.

There was something wildly reassuring about being surrounded by all these bodies, warmer even than his own.

Yu hugged them a little tighter before looking up at Mika again.

Mika was still smiling.

What was there to smile about at a time like this? And yet there he was, smiling.

"You always make that face?" asked Yu.

Mika cocked his head. "What face?"

"That idiotic look you've got right now."

"You mean a smile?"

"Yeah."

"Dunno."

"You figure the younger kids have been through enough, so you just grin and tell them everything will be alright?" asked Yu.

Mika just smiled back at him. "You'll start doing it too, soon enough. For your family's sake," he replied.

Yu felt a wave of despair wash over him.

It all seemed so overwhelmingly hopeless.

They had been captured by bloodsucking monsters. They had no way of knowing where they were being taken, or what would happen to them when they got there.

It was hopeless.

Utterly hopeless.

Life was shit, it was enough to drive anyone to suicide—or at least it should've been, but...

"...family, huh," Yu muttered softly.

He groaned at the unfamiliar feeling of the intense warmth radiating from the children.

"I...ain't got a family," he repeated, but Mika just laughed.

And eventually sleep came to the two of them as well.

Yu closed his eyes, and his mind wandered.

It was true, the world had ended today.

But he could close his eyes and dream, and when he opened them again...

"..."

Let it still be like this.

Please let it still be like this, the old world gone.

Let these children still be here, clinging to me. Telling me they need me, telling me that I'm not just a worthless demon.

I'm tired of being alone.

I'm so tired of being alone.

Later.

When Yu opened his eyes, the world was still brimming with despair.

The adults were still dead.

The apocalypse hadn't been a dream.

And Yu...

"..."

...wasn't alone anymore.

The younger children clung to his hands with frightened faces. They wrapped their arms around his legs.

One of the vampires spoke.

"As of this moment you are all livestock. You are the property of the vampires, and exist only to supply us with blood."

Some of the children who had come from places other than Hyakuya Orphanage began to wail.

"Ha...haha..."

But Yu couldn't contain a laugh.

He wasn't alone anymore.

Beside him Mika smiled, hugging the other frightened children to him.

"It's alright. It's all going to be alright," he reassured them.

Yu followed suit. "Yeah, he's right. Everything's going to be fine, I'll protect you. Someday...someday I'll get strong enough to beat up all the vampires, so don't cry."

The children stared at Yu, wide-eyed.

"You mean it?"

Of course he didn't mean it.

What could Yu do against such monsters?

But the children looked at him with unstinting belief in their eyes. "You'll get them for us?"

So Yu gave an exaggerated nod. "Of course, just you wait. I'll get rid of 'em all."

"Wow!"

"I don't know how many years it'll take, but one day, I swear, I'll send them packing," he said.

And he kept saying it.

Over and over again.

Partly to keep himself from losing faith.

Partly to sustain the other children's spirits.

And he swore an oath to himself, that he would keep repeating it until one day he actually believed it.

And so began their new life in the world of the vampires.

Chapter 3

The Japanese Imperial Demon Army

Seraph of the End

"It's gotten a little harder to see the stars," Guren muttered to himself.

With the power back on, recovery efforts had sped up dramatically.

Kureto had taken decisive action, mobilizing the children of the followers of the Order of Imperial Demons to transform Shibuya into a livable place.

They transported the endless piles of bodies out of the area to be burned.

And each time they gazed upon another burning pyre, it only strengthened their loyalty to one another.

All adults who had not submitted to the demon curse experiments were now dead; most of the survivors were young children, and it was up to them to rebuild for the sake of the other children who were younger still.

Every day, from sunup to sundown, they dragged away the bodies and offered silent prayers for them as they burned.

And so they proclaimed:

We will restore the city.

We will restore the country.

We will continue to live, here in this place.

"Hey Guren," said Kureto Hiragi, beside him.

Guren's eyes remained fixed on the sky. He didn't answer.

Kureto repeated, "Guren."

"What?"

"What are you looking at?"

"The sky, what else?"

"What is there to see in the sky?"

"The stars. They've faded a little."

"It's because of the funeral pyres."

"Yeah."

"And because you got the power back on. The night isn't quite as dark as it used to be."

It was true. Shibuya now emitted a dazzling glow all through the night.

The corpses were decaying fast, so they had to keep the fires blazing non-stop.

Guren turned away from the sky and back to the reality below. A great mountain of corpses was burning before his eyes. The smell, like barbecue mingled with scorched plastic, made his head spin.

Guren gazed into the flames for a while before speaking. "Can I go now?"

But Kureto shook his head. "Stay by my side until it's over."

"Planning to give another one of your rousing speeches?"

"Of course."

"Aren't you done with that? Everyone's heard it already. You give the same speech every day."

Kureto stared at the burning bodies as he spoke. "It's not

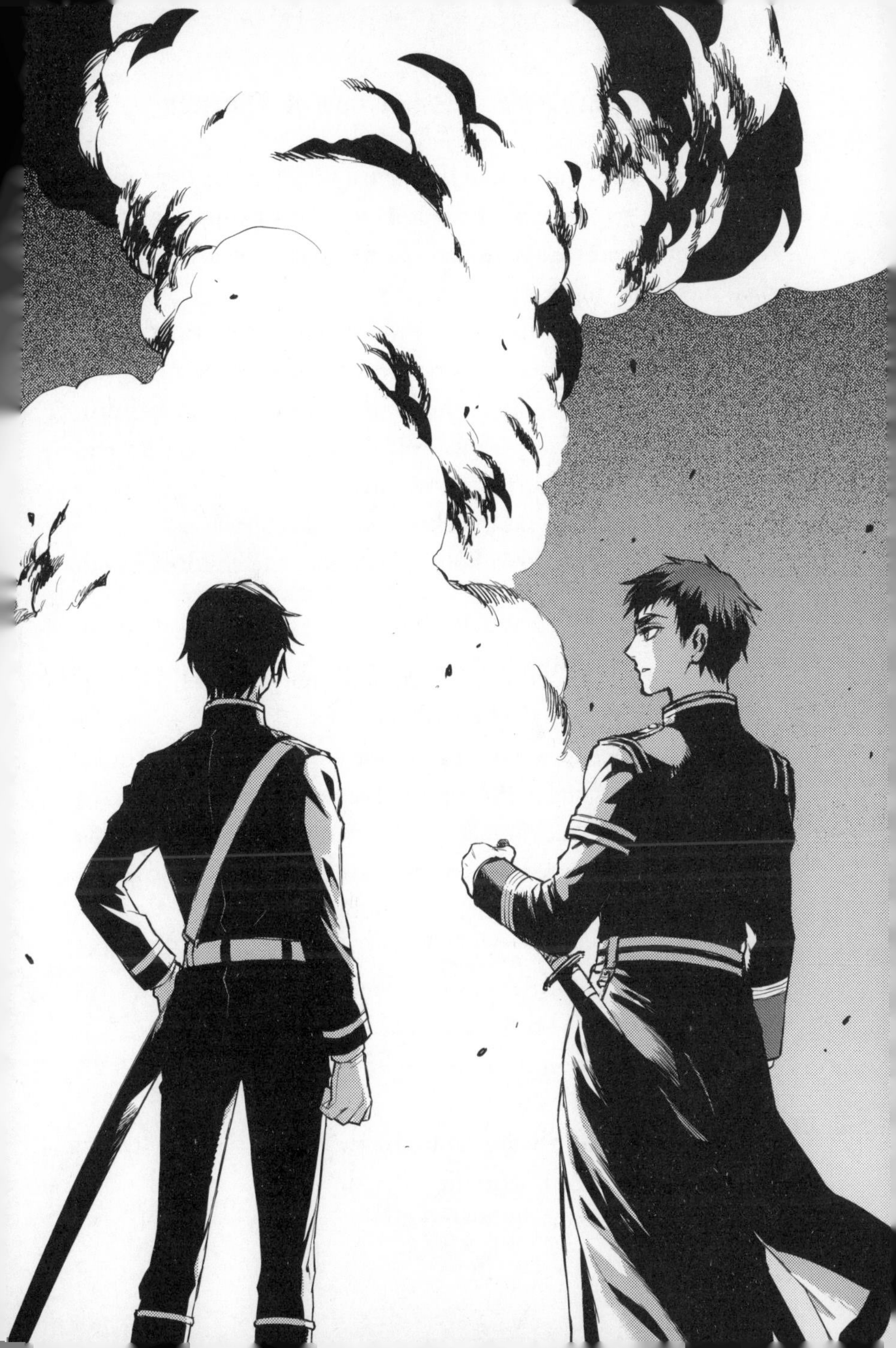

enough, not yet. They could hear me a dozen times over and it still wouldn't be enough. The world's been turned upside down. The people need to be unified, to be given purpose," he finished, taking a step forward.

Aoi Sangu waited to one side holding a microphone. Kureto took it, and his voice echoed across all of Shibuya.

Those gathered around the bodies, watching them burn, were all children. Every adult over the age of twelve who had not received the demon's curse was dead.

Someone had to lead the children, and rebuild.

At the sight of Kureto holding his mic, the children began to shout.

"Lord Kureto!"

"Everyone be quiet! Lord Kureto's about to speak!"

"Mister Popular," Guren smirked.

Kureto glanced back at him, a smile crossing his lips. "You've got plenty of fans yourself. You're the one they have to thank for getting the power back on. So stand behind me with your arms crossed and look important. We need them to look up to you."

"Hmph, you can't order me around."

Aoi glared at him. "Who do you think you're talking to? You're nothing but an Ichinose! I should kill you for that," she said, placing a hand on the sword at her waist.

"You could try," replied Guren after a pause, staring her in the eye.

"You sonofa—" She began to draw.

"Stand down, Aoi," Kureto ordered.

Aoi stared at him. "But—"

"If you're going to kill him do it somewhere else. We're trying to show a unified front, remember?"

"Yes... I remember."

"Besides, Guren doesn't mean it, not really. We no longer have any hostages. There's nothing forcing the Ichinose Clan to stand by the Hiragis anymore. And yet, here he is. Because he understands that this is exactly where he needs to be if we're going to rebuild the human race. Isn't that right, Guren?" said Kureto, almost as if he were trying to convince himself. "You're right where you need to be, at the feet of your lord."

Behind Kureto, Guren could see the children staring in their direction, their expressions beaming with pride. A sea of faces pointed their way, illuminated by the light of the fire—of the burning bodies, burning flesh, burning lives.

Life went on, even after the apocalypse.

It almost looked as if they envied Guren for getting to speak with Kureto.

What Kureto said was true.

They needed a strong leader, a guiding hand.

Someone strong enough to convince them that even the end of the world was of little consequence.

"Let's begin," said Kureto.

He brought the mic to his lips, breathed in slightly, and paused for a moment—then began his speech.

"Listen, brothers and sisters! I bring you a proclamation from the Order of the Imperial Demons, the caretakers and saviors of Shibuya."

It was the same speech he gave every day.

Guren Ichinose: Resurrection at Nineteen

"Today we have taken another step forward. We have gathered together the remains of our departed fellows, and returned them to the heavens." Kureto pointed a finger at the sky. "See how the smoke rises into the sky! As we stare into the fire, we cannot but ask ourselves, where do our fallen comrades go after they are consigned to the flames?

"In what corner of the firmament does this smoke come to rest after it drifts into the sky?

"In the old world, there were those who believed that when we die, we go to Heaven.

"And there were those who said that the wicked go instead to Hell.

"Those who went to Heaven would receive God's love.

"And those who trespassed would be punished below.

"There were many adults who said such things.

"They told us that God was watching us.

"That he was watching over us.

"But was it true?

"So many have died, the world lies in ruin, and still no God has shown himself.

"Where, then, is this God?

"*What* is God?

"I—we, the Order of the Imperial Demons, don't believe there is a Heaven waiting beyond the clouds. Nor any God above.

"For I ask you, if there is a God, how can he leave humanity to languish in such pain?" Kureto levelled his finger now at the burning corpses. "How can he leave your comrades to burn?

Your parents, your siblings, your friends, your sweethearts, what did they do to deserve such a fate? What deed could be so unforgivable that they deserved to be reduced to ash in a place like this, one body indistinguishable from the next?" Kureto demanded in a stentorian voice.

The children listened with rapt attention. Some wept. Guren couldn't blame them. Their own parents and siblings were among the burning bodies.

Kureto continued.

"There is no God.

"That is what I believe.

"There is no God.

"That is what *we* believe.

"There is no God.

"That is what *you* believe.

"There is no God.

"There is no God.

"That is what the Order of the Imperial Demons believes.

"And even if there is a God, that God will not aid us today.

"And *that* is why we must work together to rebuild this godless world.

"You, yes all of you, take each other's hands, and together we will forge a future for ourselves.

"The Order of the Imperial Demons was once the greatest religious syndicate in all of Japan. We struggled against many other religious organizations—the name of the Brotherhood of a Thousand Nights might strike a chord for some of you. Perhaps your parents even belonged to it. Or to some other organization, that worshipped its own god.

"But hear me now!" cried Kureto, pointing to the mountain of corpses. "Those organizations no longer exist. Your country, your traditions, the parents who once watched over you—they're all gone.

"Naught remains.

"Only chaos.

"Know, however, that chaos brings only death, brother killing brother. If we allow our different opinions, beliefs, and dreams to come into conflict, we will devour ourselves.

"So today we say *No more!*

"Today we commit that past to the fire, along with the bodies of our fallen fellows.

"And we, the Order of the Imperial Demons, hereby declare:

"We shall be your lords.

"We shall be the hand that guides you.

"Strange monsters roam the land, and vampires steal children in the night. But we will become a shining beacon in this dark world, to protect you, and guide you.

"And so, as of today, we will take on a new name.

"We will adopt a new mantle suitable for those who will be the leaders of all who have survived across Japan, the saviors who will rebuild this world.

"From this day forward, we shall be known as the Japanese Imperial Demon Army.

"Each survivor is a soldier now, fighting to save the world.

"If you cannot let go of your old religions yet, you may

continue to practice them for the time being.

"Believe in whatever god you wish.

"But know that as of today, you are all soldiers. Your life is pledged to your brothers and sisters.

"Where there are enemies, you shall slay them.

"Where there are vampires, you shall slay them.

"Where there are monsters, you shall slay them.

"And where there are demons, you shall subjugate them and make them serve us.

"And if there is a God, and that God proves to be our enemy—if he comes for your brothers and sisters—then we shall slay God himself!" cried Kureto, drawing his sword.

The katana which held the demon known as Raimeiki—the Thunderbringer.

A bolt of lightning shot up from the sword into the sky.

A single column of electricity that pierced the night.

There was an almost divine beauty in its dazzling light. The children raised their heads and stared, spellbound.

The display had had its desired effect.

With so little left for them to rely on, Kureto must have seemed like a new god born into the void.

His sword still thrust toward the sky, he shouted, "Hear me! Today, we become the Japanese Imperial Demon Army! You are all now soldiers of the Japanese Imperial Demon Army! Renounce your lives for the sake of your fellows! For the sake of the world!

"Today we make a stand!

"Here, in Shibuya!

"Today we light a beacon of hope!

"Raise your battle cry!

"For today we proclaim ourselves the Japanese Imperial Demon Army!

"Let me hear you!"

At this, the children raised their voices in unison.

WE ARE THE JAPANESE IMPERIAL DEMON ARMY!

WE ARE THE JAPANESE IMPERIAL DEMON ARMY!

These children, who had nowhere else to turn, shouted at the top of their lungs.

Kureto nodded, satisfied, and handed the mic back to Aoi.

He glanced toward Guren. "I thought I told you to cross your arms and look important."

Guren knew he should, for the sake of the children. Right now they needed something, anything, to believe in. It didn't matter what it was.

Guren sighed, and thrust his right fist triumphantly into the air.

The children went wild, sending up a great cheer, and began chanting even louder than before: *WE ARE THE JAPANESE IMPERIAL DEMON ARMY!*

Kureto grinned. "Excellent. Welcome to the Japanese Imperial Demon Army, Guren."

"Get bent."

"Hahaha."

"Was this your idea? Bringing together all the religions and making them all soldiers?"

"No, I'm just following orders. Apparently they tried kidnapping and brainwashing some children, and decided that this was the most effective way of going about things."

"Really stepping into your father's shoes, Lord Hiragi. You bastard."

"Yes, but it's this bastard who's going to save the world. And you're going to help me, Guren."

"…"

Kureto turned away from the crowd of children and began walking toward his car. Aoi went with him.

As he watched Kureto walk away, Guren pondered what he had just seen.

According to Kureto, there was no god.

Such was the doctrine of both the Order of the Imperial Demons and the Order of the Imperial Moon, which the Ichinose Clan had led.

God does not exist.

There is only human desire and the curse it brings.

And yet.

"…"

Guren stared at the children, who continued to chant their allegiance to the Japanese Imperial Demon Army as the pile of corpses burned.

"What is all this, if not divine punishment?" he murmured.

Guren had brought the dead back to life, and the world had come to an end.

And the end had come so suddenly, so forcefully, that it was hard to believe it could be anything other than God's wrath.

Guren had violated the taboo.

Guren Ichinose: Resurrection at Nineteen

Like the tower of Babel, or the wings of Icarus.
He didn't know if there was a God or not.
But there had definitely been divine punishment.
Suddenly, a beautiful girl alighted softly before Guren.
It was Mahiru.
She peered at him, grinning in undisguised amusement.

—Did it ever occur to you that it was punishment for sleeping with me?

"Huh?"

—Think about it, it was a forbidden love! Wanna do it again?

Mahiru was still dressed in her old sailor-suit school uniform. The hem of her shirt was riding up, and at the center of her exposed alabaster waist, Guren could see her delicate navel. Guren felt desire begin to build uncontrollably within him. Both sexual appetite—and the urge to destroy.

—Your body knows what it wants. It wants to ravage me, to kill me.

"But you only exist inside my mind. You're just a fantasy."

—I'm right here.

"For all I know you're just a hallucination created by my

demon."

—*But I am a demon.*

"How am I supposed to sleep with a fantasy, anyway?"

—*Most boys spend all their time thinking about their dirty fantasies.*

Mahiru slowly began lifting up her skirt.

"Go away."

—*Your mouth says no, but your body says yes. You don't get to seeee, though.*

"Whatever, just piss off."

—*Ahaha.*

Mahiru laughed innocently. What did she think she was doing? Why had she become a demon? Did she even really exist? None of it made sense to Guren.

"Hey Mahiru."

—*What?*

"Supposing for a moment that you do exist…"

—Supposing? Haven't I already proven it to you? I told you that vampire was coming, didn't I?

That hardly constituted proof, though. Demons were always trying to take over their human hosts. And the ones who became possessed were no longer in their right mind. As long as the demon was in the driver's seat, the host's memories were suspect. There was no way of knowing for sure what they might have done while possessed.

The information about the vampire might actually have come from Guren himself, while he was under demonic control—

—Wrong.

Mahiru cut him off.

—You're way off base.

"Don't read my thoughts."

—I can't read your thoughts, you've built a wall around your mind. If you would just lower it for a moment we could share so much more information.

"I won't let you have your way with me."

—I'd much rather you had your way with me.

Mahiru took a step closer, and Guren involuntarily took a step back.

—Haha, scaredy-cat.

"You can hardly blame me for being scared of you."
She was a certified genius, after all.
She had been leading him and Kureto and Shinya around by their noses for the last ten years, and never once, in all that time, did any of them figure out what was going on in that head of hers.
In fact, she was manipulating them even now.

—You need to conquer your fear, Guren. Humans can only grow stronger if they face their fears.

"You faced yours, and now you're not even human anymore."

—I could say the same for you.

"I'm still human."

—Ahaha.

"I am."

—*Ahahaha.*

Mahiru's laugh was somehow melancholy.
"Mahiru," Guren began, searching her face.

—*Yes?*

"How much did you know? About what Saito said, about some of his tissue being inside my ancestor's body. Assuming what he said is true, did you already know?"
Mahiru shook her head.

—*I didn't know about that. Or should I say* even *I didn't know about any of that.*

It was impossible to trust anything Mahiru said, but it seemed like she was telling the truth this time.
"Even our first encounter was planned."

—*Everything is planned.*

"It was already planned hundreds of years ago."

—*Does that make us soulmates, then?*

"It's not funny."

—Who's laughing?

It was true, she wasn't even smiling.
She looked a little pleased, maybe, but by and large her expression was inscrutable.

"Mahiru."

—Yeah?

"I'm going to lower the walls around my mind a little. I want information on—"
But Guren suddenly realized her eyes were no longer fixed on him. She was looking over his shoulder.
Someone was there.
Mahiru vanished.
Her voice, however, continued to echo inside his head.

—Later. Tonight. You can lower your walls. And then I can take off my clothes ♪

Maybe lowering those walls wasn't such a good idea after all. Mahiru was strong, and brilliant, and seductive. Guren doubted he would be able to maintain control.
She could possess him easily.
"Why does everything have to be such a fucking pain in the ass," Guren groaned, looking over his shoulder.

Shinya was standing there.

He pointed an accusing finger at Guren. "I saw you earlier. With your fist up in the air, playing hero in front of the children. Woo-woo, aren't you cool!"

"You making fun of me?"

"Of course."

"Then shaddup."

"Woo-woo-woo, Mister Big Stuff, Mister Cool—"

Guren tried to kick him, but—

"Missed me!" Shinya laughed as he dodged out of the way.

"You're cruising for a bruising."

"Ahaha," Shinya laughed.

Talking with Shinya was so easy. Sure, he was smart, and it wasn't like Guren ever knew what Shinya was thinking, either. But Guren never felt afraid of him.

He knew they were in the same boat.

Mahiru was something they had in common; they were victims of the same monster.

"Anyway," said Guren, "I thought you weren't going to come today."

Shinya nodded. "I wasn't. Kureto's been giving that same speech every day. Once more, with feeling: We are the Japanese Imperial Demon Army!"

"You've got to hand it to him, though, going out there and giving the same speech so many times."

"But it's not really the same. It's been a few days since I last heard it, and his delivery has definitely gotten better."

"It has?"

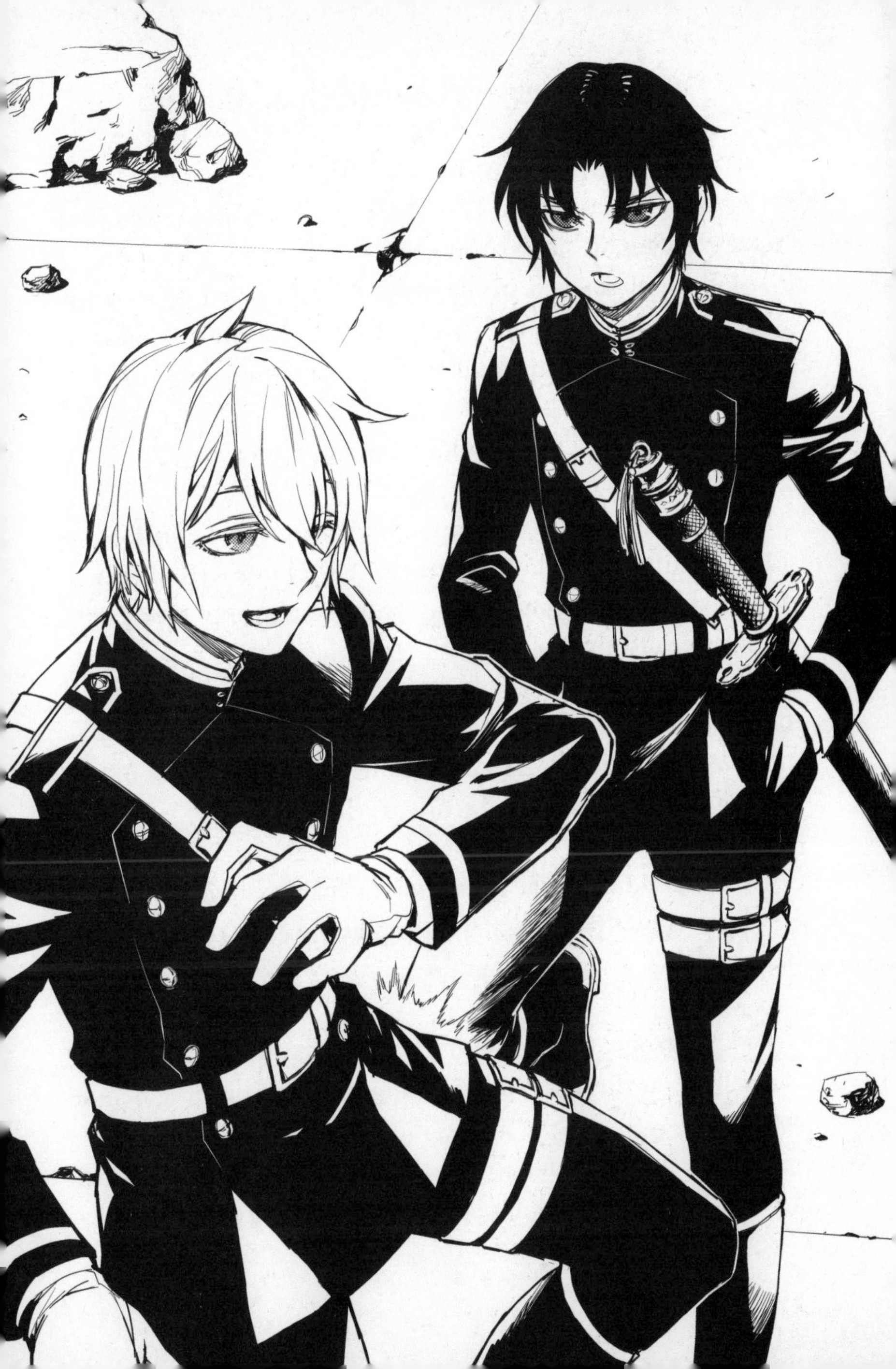

"You probably haven't noticed since you're here every day, but yeah, he's improved. I bet he secretly goes home and practices every night," joked Shinya.

Guren pictured it in his head. Kureto, holed up in a tiny room, repeating his speech over and over while he finetuned the timing of thrusting his fist into the air or minutely adjusted the angle of his sword.

"Definitely!" Guren couldn't contain himself.

"Right? My brother's so serious."

"He even did it to me. You should've seen the smug look on his face earlier when he said, get this, 'Welcome to the Japanese Imperial Demon Army, Guren!' How much you wanna bet he even practiced that—"

But Shinya burst out laughing before Guren could finish his sentence.

Seeing his face, Guren couldn't help but laugh as well.

And he felt some small sense of relief.

The sight of his friends' smiling faces always helped Guren feel like he had made the right choice when he resurrected them.

Even though he knew what a presumptuous thought that was.

"..."

How arrogant could he be, looking for reasons to forgive himself when there was a mountain of bodies burning behind him.

All the same, when he looked at Shinya's smiling face, Guren felt like he might yet be forgiven. He let out a tiny sigh of relief.

"What are you sighing for?"

Guren pointed over his shoulder. "It's the smell of the burning bodies."

Shinya turned to gaze at the pile of burning bodies.

Guren couldn't decipher what emotion might be hidden in his friend's eyes, but watching the fire dispassionately, Shinya said, "You get used to something like this eventually, when you see it every day."

"I don't."

"Fine, you never get used to it."

"Pick one!" retorted Guren.

Shinya just shrugged his shoulders and smiled sadly. He was quiet for a moment, before his usual smile returned. "Anyway, forget about that!"

Forget about the burning bodies of their friends, family, lovers—and find something positive to think about.

Shinya went on. "Did you hear all that fuss Norito was making about his big discovery?"

"His what?"

"You mean you haven't heard? At breakfast he was making a huge deal about some 'really important discovery.'"

"I didn't eat breakfast today."

"You didn't? What were you doing?"

"What do you think? I was out tilling the fields on the east side of Shibuya."

"Hunting monsters, you mean?"

"Yeah. Speaking of which, you were supposed to be out there too."

"I know."

"Then where were you!"

"I was sleepy!" laughed Shinya. But actually he'd had a good excuse. He and Norito had been called out in the middle of the night by the squad building the wall to stop the monsters coming in from the north.

The monsters were strong. Every night they lost a few more comrades.

But slowly, slowly, the Japanese Imperial Demon Army was beginning to find ways of beating them back.

Ways of drawing even greater power from their cursed gear.

And training methods to ensure that those with the necessary aptitude were able to use the new weapons effectively.

Developing these weapons required human experimentation, of course, but fortunately there was no shortage of volunteers.

Everyone was ready to put their lives on the line for the sake of their friends and comrades.

This may have stemmed from weakness, from a desire to run from what the world had become and escape into oblivion, but either way, they were united in one purpose.

A desire to become stronger.

Even a little bit stronger, if it meant they could protect their friends.

They had lost enough already. They couldn't stand to lose any more. So they had to get stronger, in order to protect the friends they had left.

Some of the children came to Guren and asked him to teach them how to use a sword.

Some came to ask for magical training.

But such rudiments availed them nothing against the monsters. Children he met one day would be slaughtered before his eyes the very next.

Guren vowed that the next time would be different. He began to dedicate all of his spare time to training the children.

Little boys and girls who had never even heard the word "sorcery" were training every day, and putting their lives on the line against the monsters.

That was why the Hiragis called them an army.

The Japanese Imperial Demon Army.

It was just a reflection of reality.

There were no civilians anymore.

"How're things coming on the north?" asked Guren.

Guren was in charge of the eastern border.

Shinya, the northern.

And Kureto, the western and southern borders.

"It's pretty bad," replied Shinya. "But they're starting to learn."

Shinya was training the children in his care as well.

"And we finished the wall, so hopefully we won't be losing so many people."

"Is a wall like that really going to help? Some of those creatures are strong enough to smash through it without—"

Shinya cut him off. "They said they can create a barrier to stop the powerful creatures from getting too close."

"And you believe 'em?"

"They said they would put the barrier up once the wall was

finished."

"When?"

"I don't know."

"I don't know isn't good enough. My people are dropping like flies out there."

"It's the same on the north."

"We should make Kureto give us some answers."

"My brother probably wishes more than anyone that they'd hurry up. He's handling both south *and* west," said Shinya, beginning to walk away.

Guren walked with him.

Some of the children stared as they passed, their eyes filled with admiration. But how many of them would still be alive tomorrow?

Things did seem to be getting a little better every day, however. Though they were starting from so far in the red that every improvement seemed like a miracle.

They were all getting stronger.

Shinya climbed onto a dirt bike parked a little way away, then glanced over his shoulder at Guren.

"How did you get here?"

"In Kureto's car."

"Want a ride?"

"Sure," replied Guren, climbing onto the back of the bike. Shinya started the engine, which growled out a low thrum.

"Alright, let's go. Hold on tight."

"Shut up."

And they were off.

Into the night.

Racing through the wasteland of their fallen world on the back of a motorbike.

There was no need for helmets anymore. All the police officers who might have pulled them over for riding without a helmet had been killed by the virus.

With the power back on, the traffic lights were working again, but no one obeyed them. They would probably get turned off before long.

But some things never change.

The dark of night, for instance, or the feel of the wind in your hair.

Guren could feel the heat coming off Shinya's back.

It was a reminder that his friend was still alive.

Guren increased the demon's strength slightly and strained his ears. He could hear Shinya's blood pumping and his heart beating beneath the sound of the rushing wind. Again, Guren felt as if he had done the right thing in bringing Shinya back.

That he had made the right choice, even if the world had ended.

" . . . "

Guren listened to Shinya's heartbeat as he watched the ruins speed past.

Ba-bump. Ba-bump. Ba-bump. Shinya's heart thumped out a steady rhythm.

Ba-bump. Ba-bump. Ba-bump. It seemed to be beating a little faster than Guren's own. Probably because Shinya was doing the driving.

"Guren."

Ba-bump. Ba-bump. Ba-bump.

"Guren."

"Yeah?"

"About what I was saying earlier…"

"Earlier?"

"About Norito."

"Oh, his big discovery. With Norito, you know it's just going to be something silly."

"You're probably right," laughed Shinya.

Guren continued to count the beats of Shinya's heart. It had been fifty beats since he started.

Fifty-one. Fifty-two. Fifty-three. Supposedly the resurrection would only keep them alive for ten years. Guren wondered how many heartbeats that was.

"You've got to hand it to Norito, though," said Shinya. "The way he keeps that smile on his face, despite everything that's happened. It probably gives a lot of people the courage to get through the day."

"Yeah, I guess."

"When you think about it, he really is a grownup."

"Hahaha," Guren burst out laughing uncontrollably. The words "Norito" and "grownup" just didn't seem to go together. But he had to admit… "You're right."

Guren stopped counting Shinya's heartbeats, and instead began to wonder what Norito's big discovery could be.

If it were Mito, for instance, it would almost certainly be something to do with games.

Sayuri was all about cooking.

And Shigure… Well, she was a harder nut to crack. It wasn't easy to say what she was into. Guren had asked her once about the best way to conceal a weapon, though, and her face had lit up as she launched into a thorough explanation.

But Norito—Guren gave it some thought.

"I bet it's something dirty," he said finally.

Shinya nodded. "Knowing him, probably."

"A dirty magazine?"

"No, he made a big deal about finding one of those the day before yesterday. He said this was his greatest find yet."

"Do you think he finally found a porno?"

"Hahaha, maybe. You ever seen a porno before, Guren?"

"Have you?"

"I asked first."

"You answer first."

"Come on, just tell me," coaxed Shinya.

"Even if I had," said Guren, glancing around as he spoke, "all the men and women who were in it would be dead now."

All of the adults had died, after all.

And it was Guren's fault.

Because he had brought Shinya, Norito, Mito, Shigure, and Sayuri back to life.

"You know what Norito would say if he heard that," said Shinya, laughing. "*What a waste!*"

"What a waste?"

"Can't you picture him saying that?"

"Yeah, I guess I can. A waste, huh…"

Guren Ichinose: Resurrection at Nineteen

Lost in conversation, they soon passed through the unfinished wall hastily being built around Shibuya. Once inside, they sped toward the building that had become the official barracks of the Japanese Imperial Demon Army.

Chapter 4

Two Geniuses

Seraph of the End

The time was 9:15 p.m.

Lights out for off-duty children ten and under was 9:00.
For the older kids it was at 10:00.
So the youngest children should've already been in bed, safe and sound.
As they walked down the hall, however, there were still children excitedly scampering to and fro.
"What the hell?" muttered Guren, as he watched them running every which way.
"Uh-oh, it's Second Lieutenant Guren!"
"It's Second Lieutenant Ichinose!"
"Crap, we're busted!" the children cried in a panic. They were so young they probably didn't even know what the words "second lieutenant" meant.
Second lieutenant. Guren's current rank.
Not that the title held much meaning. Now that they were officially an army, Guren had been made a lieutenant only because there weren't enough adults left to fill the role. Even then, he had only been given that rank grudgingly, thanks to his role in getting the power back on, and because he had Kureto's

backing. The truth, however, was that the top brass still thought of him as an Ichinose traitor.

For proof, Guren need look no further than Norito and Mito, who had both been made lieutenant colonels.

Shinya, meanwhile, was a full-blown colonel.

But all that stuff about rank went over the children's heads. Doubtless the Hiragis would begin using rank and title to control and motivate their troops before too long, but now wasn't the time for that. Right now everyone was still focused on working together to survive.

"What's all the ruckus?" Guren asked, but the children just blushed and ran away.

Guren watched them flee, then looked over at Shinya.

"What do you think that was all about?"

"Norito's discovery, maybe?"

The uproar only increased the farther down the hall they went—children screaming and hollering, all of them boys.

"Can I go back to my room now?" asked Guren, staring at the scene through heavy lids.

Shinya laughed. "Norito said he wanted you there too."

"I'll pass."

"Come on, you know you want to see it."

"Who would want to see something like that with such a crowd?"

"Oh, I see. So you'd rather sneak back here in the middle of the night and watch it all alone?"

"Well… I mean, if I *was* going to watch it, wouldn't that make the most sense? So it's settled, then. I'll just come back later," Guren finished, turning to head back to his room, when a voice suddenly stopped him.

"Hey, Guren, where do you think you're going? You're not gonna believe what I found. You've gotta come see this!"

It was Norito, yelling to them from the end of the hall.

He was poking his head out of the room where all the kids had gathered, waving them over.

"They're gonna charge you with corrupting public morals," said Guren.

"What makes you think I'm corrupting public morals?"

"Your whole existence is a corruption of public morals."

"Just get over here," insisted Norito, "It's nothing like that, I promise."

True, Norito had never said his big discovery was a porno. Maybe it really was something innocent.

"Guess it's not a video, after all," Guren said to Shinya.

"Maybe it's a smutty novel, then."

"Do you really think these little brats would be so worked up over a book?"

"What else could it be? An eroge, maybe?"

"What's an eroge?"

"An erotic game."

"How can a game be erotic?"

"Don't ask me."

"Don't lie, you must've played one before."

"Come on, let's just take a look already. Maybe Norito will surprise us."

"Are we really gonna do this?" groaned Guren, trailing after

Shinya down the hall.

The whole hallway was packed with children, who all looked up as they passed.

"Oh, it's Lord Guren!"

"And Lord Shinya!"

"Clear a path! They've come to see the treasure!"

"Everyone, look! Lord Guren and Lord Shinya are here to see the treasure!"

"They're here! They're here! They're here to see the treasure!" the children shouted.

"If this turns out to be a porno, I swear I'm going to kill Norito," said Guren.

Shinya grinned. "What's wrong with having a little fun?"

"Plenty."

"It's not like there's a lot of fun left to be had in this world."

"Tough shit," said Guren. The words were barely out of his mouth before he realized what was waiting for them inside the room.

They could hear loud voices drifting from the open door at the end of the hall.

"Ahh, no, dooon't."

"Yeah baby, you like that? Does it make you feel dirty?"

"Doooooon't, stop, no, don't stop! Stop it—"

Guren buried his face in his hands.

He trudged towards the room.

There were about two dozen kids packed inside like sardines.

They were all sitting cross-legged, staring at a TV.

The screen must've been 50 inches across.

On that 50-inch screen, a balding middle-aged man was tormenting a woman who looked to be in her late thirties.

"…"

Sitting there in the middle of the crowd of children was Norito, wearing a serious expression.

He glanced over his shoulder at Guren, and pointed toward the 50-inch TV.

"Right?" he said.

"What's right?" Guren shot back.

Norito rolled his eyes, as if it should have been obvious. "This!"

"What about it?"

"Pretty impressive, right?"

"Looks like I was right about the corruption of public morals."

"Corruption? This is a rare treasure, you philistine."

"I dare you to say that to Mito," Guren fumed. "More importantly, listen up you little shits! What the hell are you all doing in here, it's past your bedtime!"

The children bolted to their feet.

"S-Sorry, sir!!"

"L-Lord Goshi said it was alright!"

"Calm down, you nincompoops. Lord Guren just wants to watch the treasure by himself."

"Oh, of course. Sorry, Lord Guren. We'll just come back later, then…"

Guren Ichinose: Resurrection at Nineteen

"No, no, NOOOOOOOO!" screamed Guren. "I have no intention of watching it! I'm angry because you're breaking the rules. Some of you definitely aren't eleven yet. Lights out was half an hour ago!"

In response, the children who were clearly too young to be up scrambled out of the room.

"No fair, the adults get to have all the fun."

"Shut up, they'll hear you. Remember what Lord Goshi said, we can just come back later."

The children were still smiling and laughing as they left the room, however, like children making their way home from a festival. Guren narrowed his eyes as he watched them go.

He had to admit that it might not be so bad if they had a little fun. There was so little amusement left in the world now.

"Did you hear what those kids said? *The adults* get to have all the fun," chuckled Shinya. "Someone should tell them we're only sixteen…"

Norito grinned. "Either way, now that the kids are gone it's time for the adults to play. Who wants to go first?"

"Count me out." Guren's exasperation was boiling over.

"What? Why?"

"Just forget it. Besides, these ladies are old."

At which Norito pulled several more DVDs out of his inside pocket. "I knew you'd say that. That's why I also brought some barely legal—"

"That's not what I meant!"

"Then perhaps I can interest you in some amateur couples, you know, hidden camera stuff—"

"Amateur couples?" Shinya broke in.

"Don't encourage him," seethed Guren, but Norito pretended not to hear.

"Yes indeed, my fine sir. I had you pegged as a connoisseur. Then it's decided. Tonight we feast on hidden camera couples!" he exclaimed, eagerly walking over to put in the DVD.

Guren looked at Shinya skeptically. "Are you seriously into this?"

Shinya shrugged. "I was just wondering if it's really done with hidden cameras or if it's all staged."

"Suuuuure."

"What do you think?"

"I think I don't give a shit."

Staged or not, everyone who appeared in the video was dead now thanks to the virus.

Norito finally pressed PLAY.

"Here we go!"

The name of a company—presumably the one that had made the film—floated into view on the 50-inch screen. Next, the title card appeared:

*100% Real!!! Hidden Cam Couple F*c*fest!!!*

"Oh shit, guys, this is *100% real*," Norito crowed.

"Dumbass," Guren shot back sardonically, but the movie was already starting.

It opened on a scene in downtown Shibuya.

Guren Ichinose: Resurrection at Nineteen

It looked like it might be a Sunday; the famous Shibuya Scramble bustled with a massive crowd. Guren was pretty sure it had been the busiest intersection in the world.

How many of the people on the screen had been among the corpses they had burned earlier on the outskirts of Shibuya? Surely none of them had suspected in that moment that the world was about to end.

The camera focused in on a couple enjoying their day out.

"I want ice cream," said the girl.

Guren had never heard such wooden delivery. So much for "100% Real."

"I'm going to bed," he announced.

"Hold on, Guren," said Norito, flustered. "Just wait a little bit more. I don't blame you for being upset, I know how committed you are to authenticity. But it's still too early to give up."

"What the hell are you talking about?"

"Well, maybe they've just started going out, and they're still nervous around each other."

"You're so full of shit."

"Just give it a little while longer. I made tea and everything," said Norito.

Talk about coming prepared. Shinya took a cup from Norito and sat down cross-legged.

"You're sitting down?!"

"I mean, it would be rude not to drink it."

"Hmph." Guren glanced at his own cup, then sat down as well.

Norito joined them.

Seraph of the End

The three boys sat together amid the ruins of their world, watching the 100% *not* real amateur hidden camera porno.

"Forget ice cream, let's go to a hotel," said the guy.

"No way, we just met up!"

"But love hotels are cheaper during the day."

"No! I want a proper date. I want to go out for ice cream!"

"We can get ice cream at a convenience store. I don't have that much money today. Come on, you understand, don't you baby? Don't you?"

"Do you even have enough money for a hotel?"

"..."

"Oh my god, seriously?!"

"We can go to my house instead. My family's out today, we'll have the whole place to ourselves."

"Gross, your room's always so dirty."

"Come on, don't be like that, baby."

"I guess it's starting to get a little more real," remarked Shinya as the scene unfolded.

"Right? Besides, it said it right there on the screen: 100% Real. So it's gotta be true."

"Think about it for a sec. Who's filming it, then?"

"I bet it was the brother. He probably has cameras planted all over the house."

"I can't believe you," protested the girl, before giving in. *"Fine, whatever."*

The scene faded to black.

"Finally, now for the good stuff," Norito exulted.

But when the scene finally changed the couple were in a convenience store, enthusiastically picking out flavors of ice cream.

"Was this scene really necessary?" asked Guren.

"Can't wait for the action, can you, you pervert?" replied Shinya.

"Yeah, Guren. Scenes like this are what make the payoff worth it."

"If you say so."

The three sipped at their tea.

Just then, a girl's voice came from behind them.

"What are you guys watching?"

"Huh?!"

Guren whirled around, only to be confronted by the sight of Mito. He had thought she was out on some mission, but here she was dressed in pajamas or sweatpants or something. She had evidently just taken a shower, and was drying her damp hair with a towel.

"What? This? This is nothing," said Norito, a little panicked.

"*I can't believe you don't even have enough money for ice cream. You're such a jerk, Masaki,*" said the girl on the screen.

Mito sat down next to the boys.

"What is this, a movie?" she asked, but Norito was still at a loss for words.

Guren shrugged. "Apparently it's a documentary about couples."

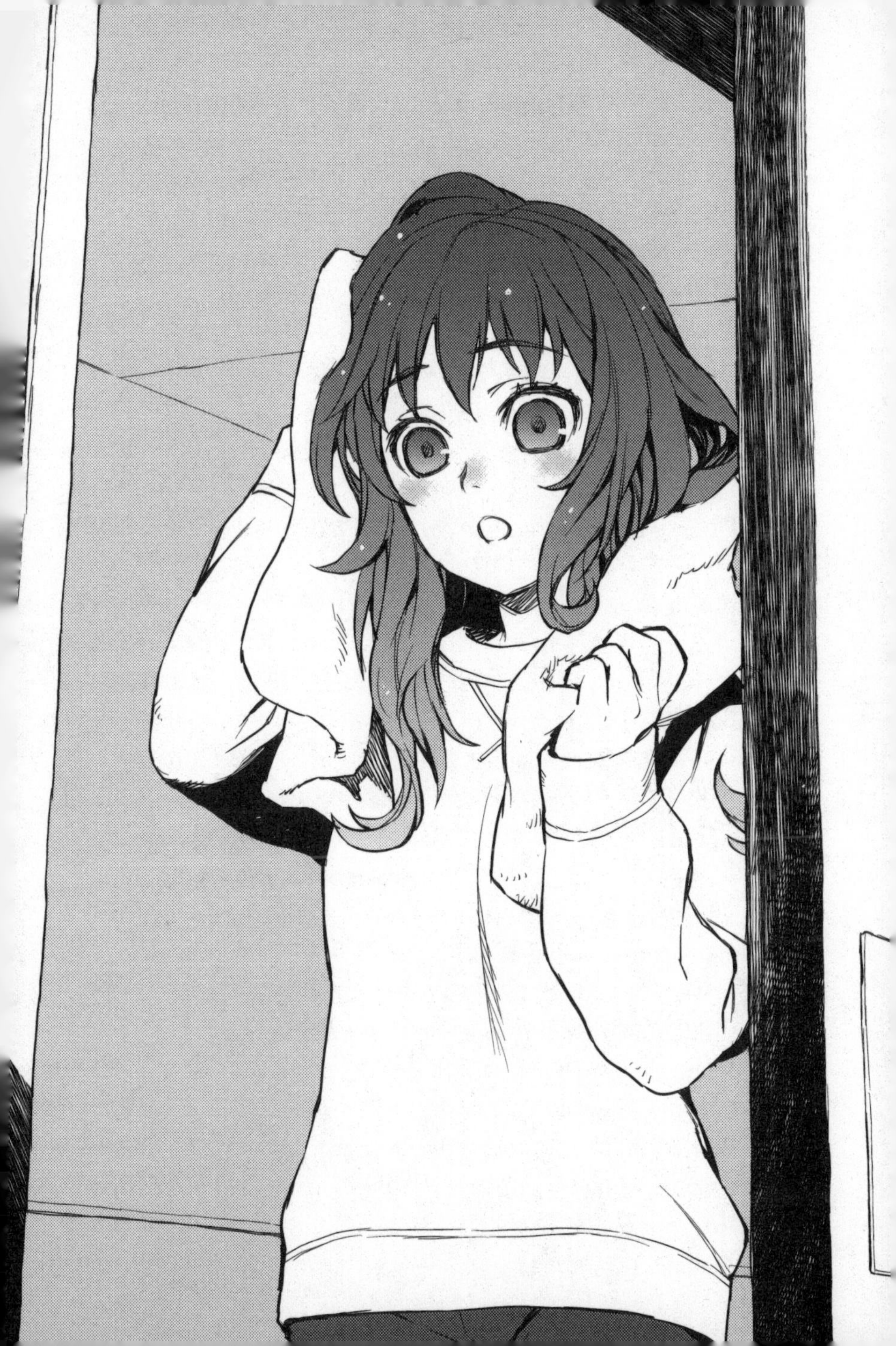

Guren Ichinose: Resurrection at Nineteen

"A documentary? That's weird, why does it seem like they're reading off a teleprompter, then?"

Guren flashed Shinya and Norito a triumphant look, but they were both clearly avoiding his gaze.

"Can't you pay for my ice cream too, Misaki? Pretty please?"

"No way! I barely got any shifts at work this month."

"Pretty, pretty please! I blew all my money at the pachinko parlor, I'm totally broke!"

"Shh! Keep your voice down, we're in a convenience store!"

"What a loser," observed Mito.

"You have to admit, though, as pointless as this scene is, it does give a sense of realism," said Shinya. "In a way, it's actually a pretty good script."

"How can it be real if there's a script?" asked Guren.

"Hahaha. Script or not, who cares? Either way, it's making me want ice cream."

"I know!" said Mito. "I was just thinking the same thing."

"Ice cream, huh?" added Norito. "You know, we could probably make some if we wanted. The next time we're out maybe we should see if we can find the ingredients."

The four looked on as the girl bought her loser boyfriend a 100-yen bar of ice cream. While they were watching, Shigure and Sayuri showed up as well.

Guren had been under the impression that they were also out on a mission, guarding a supply transfer to the southwest.

But now here they were too, wearing pajamas and looking

like they had just showered.

"Master Guren, we're back!" said Sayuri.

"We've returned, Master Guren," dittoed Shigure. "What are you watching?"

"Apparently it's a documentary," Mito responded. "Something about the everyday lives of couples."

"Oh?" The two sat down next to them.

Which meant...

"..."

...that there were now three boys and three girls, all sitting around a 50-inch TV watching *100% Real!!! Hidden Cam Couple *u*kfest!!!*

"..."

By this point, the boys were desperate for a way out. Someone had to do something before things went too far.

The movie was already starting to drift into dangerous territory.

Inside the boyfriend's house.

A kotatsu had been left out even though it was summer, and the boy and girl sat around it eating their ice cream. The scene seemed to drag on forever.

The couple looked like they were having fun. The acting might have been stiff and wooden at first, but their dialogue was slowly growing more natural.

Once the boy finished eating his ice cream he scooted over next to the girl.

She leaned against his shoulder.

Uh-oh, here we go—but no sooner had the thought occurred to Guren than Shinya suddenly spoke up:

"You know, guys, this is apparently one of Guren's favorite movies."

"What?!"

"Oh, yeah, that's right!" put in Norito. "What was your favorite scene again, Guren?"

"You bastards."

"This is your favorite?" asked Mito, turning to Guren. "I had no idea you liked documentaries."

"This is the first time I've ever heard about you liking anything, Master Guren," said Sayuri. "I can't wait to see what happens next, I'm sure it'll be fascinating!"

Shigure suddenly sat up straight and began paying close attention to the screen. "I won't miss a single minute."

"Shit."

They'd gotten him. It was too late to say anything now. If he was going to claim innocence, he should have done it right away—

"Can I kiss you?"

"Okay."

The guy on the screen leaned in and kissed the girl. Soon they were entwining their tongues eagerly, making sloppy squelching noises.

"Wha?!" cried Mito, Shigure, and Sayuri in unison.

They stared slack-jawed at the screen for a long moment, as if they couldn't believe what they were seeing. Then, again:

"Wha?!"

Their faces flushed beet red.

The events on screen had already gotten horribly out of control.

"Guren!" shouted Mito, her cheeks crimson.

"Onono," shrieked Sayuri, covering her face with her hands. She peeked out between her fingers, however, doing her best to continue watching.

"So this is what Master Guren likes. This is his…" Shigure's face was bright red, but she was still watching as closely as before, trying to maintain a dignified pose. On screen, the boyfriend had skillfully removed the girl's bra and was just about to—

"THAT'S ENOOOOOOOOOUGH!" screamed Mito, kicking the 50-inch TV across the room.

Mito had been born into the illustrious Jujo Clan, whose unique style of magic, known as the Crimson Halo, boosted the user's physical abilities. Combined with the demon's curse, a kick from Mito was no laughing matter: the TV sailed clear across the room and embedded itself in the wall.

"Explain yourself, Guren!"

But Guren, too, was at a loss.

"Shame on you, Guren," chided Shinya. He looked like he was thoroughly enjoying himself. "Showing that sort of thing to the girls."

Norito nodded vigorously. "Yeah, Guren. Shame on you and your nasty fetishes. Not that I don't see the appeal, mind you."

"B-But," stammered Sayuri, "I'm sure Master Guren has his

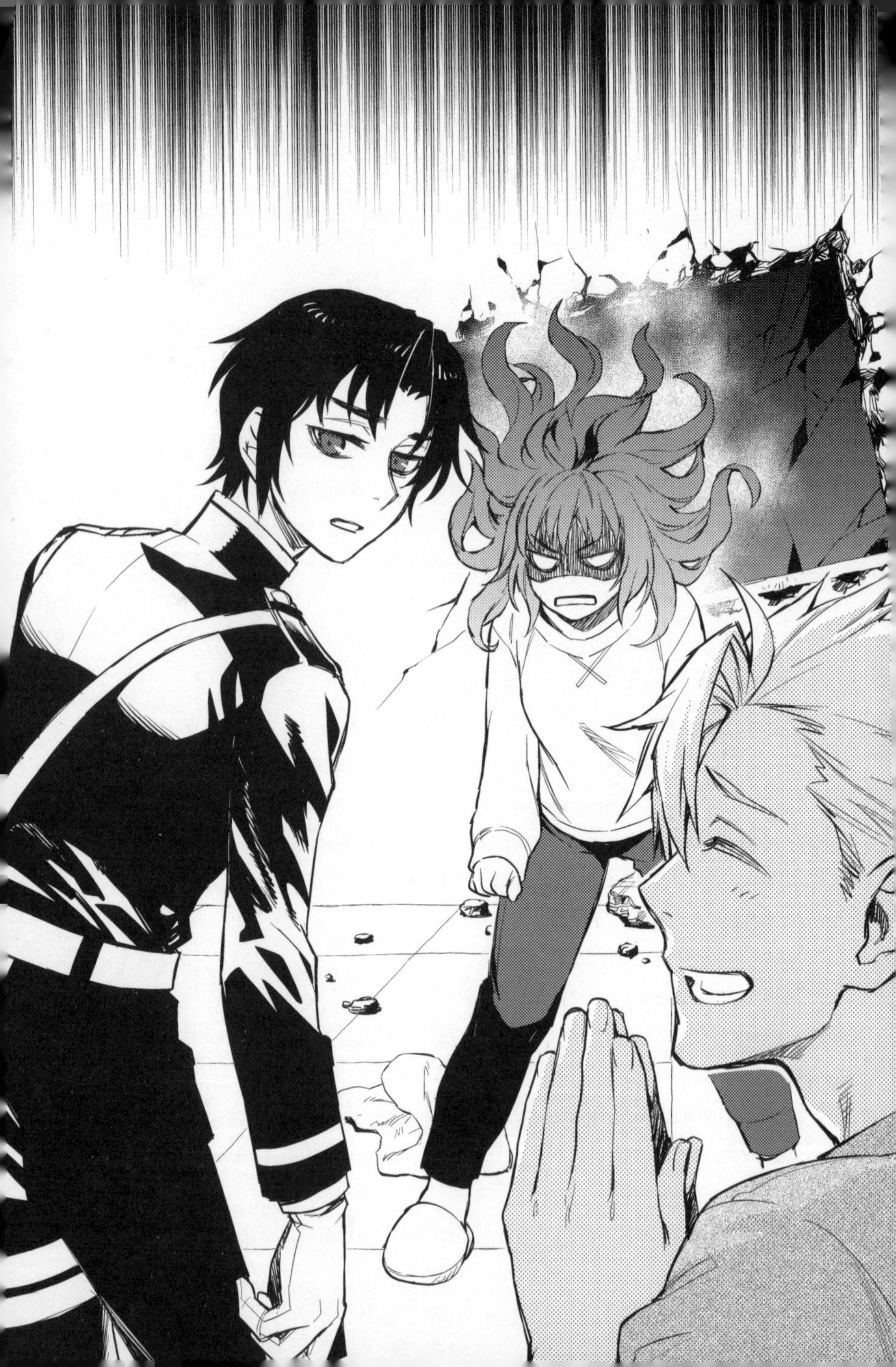

reasons. Isn't that right, Master Guren?"

Shigure nodded in agreement.

They all turned toward Guren, staring expectantly.

What was he supposed to say?

"I'm waiting, Guren," Mito demanded. Guren tried to think of something to say.

"..."

It wasn't too long ago that Mito and the others had been dead, and yet now here they were, full of life and making a stupid fuss about some dumb movie.

The silliness of it all...

"..."

...suddenly struck Guren as the most meaningful thing in the world. Tears welled up in his eyes, catching him off guard.

He didn't know why.

Maybe he was just tired.

Or maybe it was because he was weak. Such a weakling that he needed to attach special significance to the lives of his friends so he wouldn't have to face up to his responsibility for destroying the world.

Noticing the tears in his eyes, Mito began to ask, "Um, Guren..." but he played it off with a yawn. He was just tired, they were just the involuntary tears that accompany a yawn.

It wasn't weakness.

Definitely not weakness.

"Geez, I'm beat. Time to hit the hay. Got an early start again tomorrow."

"A yawn? That's all you've got?!"

"You must be tired too."

"How am I supposed to sleep unless I get a decent explanation from you?!"

"Don't ask me. I'm gonna sleep like a baby."

"No, explain yourself! What was the meaning of...that!" Mito thrust a finger at the demolished TV.

Guren didn't see why it mattered anymore, but when he looked at Norito, his friend wore a pleading expression, like he was begging Guren not to tell Mito the truth. Honestly, Guren doubted it really made a difference to Norito, either. At the end of the day Norito was a grownup, he'd be the first to step up and take responsibility in any situation that mattered—the type of guy who would lay down his life for others.

He was only making that face because it was funnier this way.

When Guren glanced at Shinya, he was still sporting the same amused grin. Come to think of it, Shinya was the one who had dragged Guren to Norito's Triple-X film festival in the first place.

Had it been a trap the whole time? Maybe Norito and Shinya had been in on it together.

As a plot to put a smile on Guren's grumpy, frowning face.

Something silly, to make him laugh.

Something meaningless.

Because if life had no meaning...

"...then you might as well laugh about it?" Guren wondered aloud, looking over at Shinya, who was, as ever, grinning back at him.

"Let's hear it, Guren," he prompted. "A convincing reason why you would show us something like that. And it better be interesting."

This was starting to get ridiculous. Seriously? If Norito and Shinya thought Guren was going to play along with this idiocy...

"Hmm."

...they were right. Guren crossed his arms and began to ponder.

Something interesting...

Something interesting...

Nothing was coming to him, but finally Guren came up with an answer.

"Guys... The truth is, if you watch for another hour, I'm in the movie."

"Wha?!" the three girls cried again in shock.

"Y-You're joking," said Mito.

"It's the truth."

"No way..."

"W-What do you mean, *in* the movie?" asked Sayuri, her voice shaking.

"I play Masaki's brother. I get naked."

"Whaaaaaa?!"

Shinya and Norito doubled over with laughter, clutching their sides.

Apparently they approved of Guren's answer.

He nodded emphatically. "If you want to see my scene, fast forward another hour. My youthful indiscretion, memorialized on video…"

Shigure spoke up, her face serious. "Th-This is a joke. Isn't it, Master Guren?"

Guren answered just as seriously. "No, it's true."

"But why would you do it?"

"For the money."

"That doesn't make any sense. You're teasing us, aren't you?"

Guren pulled a face, as if he was displeased that she refused to believe him.

Shigure flinched. "F-Forgive me, Master Guren," she said. "I would never doubt you. Alright, we'll fast forward one hour. Sayuri?"

"Huh?"

"We have to watch that tape."

"What? Why? I don't want to, I'll be scarred for life."

"It's only a movie. We're going to watch the scene."

The two girls actually walked over to the DVD player, which had been dragged along by its cord when the TV went flying, and ejected the disc.

"Wait, wait, you two are really going to watch it? There's no way Guren is really in it, is there?!" Mito asked, goggling at Guren and the girls in turn. Guren ignored them all, however, and turned on his heel to leave.

He couldn't believe the three women were really thinking about watching the rest of the movie by themselves.

Well, whatever.

He stepped out of the room and began walking down the hallway.

Shinya joined him.

"…"

"Hey Guren."

"Yeah?"

"Didn't I see you start to cry back there?"

"That was a yawn."

"It looked like you were welling up *before* you yawned."

"I was holding back the yawn the whole time."

"Oh?"

"Yep."

"*Oh?*"

"What."

"Nothing. It's just, if something's bothering you—"

Guren interrupted him. "Look around. Who doesn't have something bothering them?"

"Yeah, fair enough… Still, seemed like an odd time to cry."

"Maybe I was crying because you two were bullying me."

"We weren't bullying you."

"The worst bullies are the ones who don't realize they're bullies."

"We really weren't bullying you."

"Fuck off."

"Hahaha."

"Isn't your room in the other direction?"

"Yup."

"You've got another early day tomorrow, don't you? Go get some sleep."

"Come on, tell me."

"Tell you what?"

"Why you were crying."

It didn't seem like Shinya was going to give up. He seemed to have a sixth sense when it came to this kind of stuff.

Guren looked over at his friend.

Shinya was wearing his usual relaxed grin. But if Guren said the wrong thing, Shinya might disappear forever.

Shinya could never know that Guren had started to cry because he had suddenly found meaning in bringing his friends back to life.

"You don't give up, do you," Guren muttered.

Shinya shrugged. "Something happen while you were on duty?"

Guren could spin some simple lie, but Shinya might investigate. So what should he say? He needed to come up with a reason for crying. Something Shinya would believe, something that would explain a moment of weakness.

Maybe—

"…"

Shinya suddenly looked away from Guren. "Any chance *that's* what's been bothering you?"

That? Guren followed Shinya's gaze.

To the end of the hallway.

Where a boy was standing—

He looked to be about fourteen or fifteen. Average height and build, short black hair. And a cursed weapon strapped to his waist.

Guren looked him up and down.

"Are you the punk who's been strutting around acting like king shit?" the boy demanded. "Are you Guren Ichinose?"

"I don't recall doing any strutting," Guren answered quietly.

"You're just a lowly Ichinose, you've got some nerve acting like you're someone who matters."

This again.

No matter how strong Guren became or how much he accomplished, there were some people who would never accept him. All because he was an Ichinose, and once, long ago, the Ichinoses had betrayed the Hiragis. There was always another one of these guys, just around the corner.

Guren responded like he always did: "Yeah, you're right. Sorry about that. I'll be more careful next time."

"Cut the shit. You think you can just brush me off? Are you trying to make me look like an asshole?"

"A lowly Ichinose like myself would never dream of—"

"I knew it, you're trying to make me look like an asshole!" the boy shouted angrily.

"Ugh," whispered Shinya. "Another pain in the ass."

"Can't you get rid of him, O Lord Hiragi?" Guren whispered back.

Shinya obligingly took a step forward. "Listen, kid, I think there's been a misunderstanding."

But the boy completely ignored him. "Guren Ichinose! Let's step outside and see how strong you really are!"

"…"

Instead of answering, Guren looked over at Shinya again. Shinya just waved him along.

"Really? You're not gonna help me out here?" Guren asked incredulously.

Shinya laughed. "I've already helped you out with these guys three times."

"Yeah, but two of those times I ended up having to fight them anyway."

"Sure, but they all join your fan club after you beat them. Go on, recruit another one right now!"

"When's it gonna be your turn?"

"Lord Hiragi doesn't need fans," Shinya shot back with a yawn that made his eyes water.

"Now who's crying? Is something bothering you?"

Shinya laughed. "Yeah, I just found out that my best friend was in a porno."

"Piss off."

"Haha."

"Are you fucking kidding me?!" the boy shouted, incensed. "Don't you dare ignore me! I want you outside, now! I'll see for myself how strong you really are! I bet you've just been faking it all along!"

Chuckling, Shinya departed for his own room.

Guren returned his gaze to the boy, who was still gesticulating for Guren to follow.

"Dammit, how many of these idiots am I gonna have to deal with," Guren groaned as he headed outside.

◆

Outside the barracks.

There was an open space in front of the building that was usually reserved for training.

The boy had brought several of his friends. They all looked to be about fourteen or fifteen years old.

Guren could tell from the way the boy moved and carried himself that he had undergone extensive training. He could likely use magic as well. Not like the kids who'd been rushed through their training and had cursed gear suddenly thrust into their hands.

The boy turned around to face Guren.

His eyes were like ice. All trace of his earlier brash temper was gone.

It appeared to be an ambush. A magical trap was clearly in place around the boy.

Guren scanned the area, careful not to let the boy see that he had noticed his trap.

A voice came from behind—no, from inside Guren's head.

—These kids are stronger than you expected.

It was Mahiru.
Guren answered her silently, inside his head.
"Yeah, I noticed."

—Think you can handle it?

"I guess we'll see."

Guren Ichinose: Resurrection at Nineteen

—You mean you might lose?

"Would you give up on me if I did?"

—I'm not sure there's anything you could do to make me stop loving you, Guren.

"Hmph." Guren was speaking to the demon inside his mind.

If Mahiru was just a hallucination, then Guren must have already lost his mind. Unless he had lost it long ago, the moment he decided to bring Shinya and the others back to life.

"Well? Let's see what you've got," the boy prodded, staring at Guren.

"What's the point?" asked Guren in reply.

"I want to see what an Ichinose is made of."

"And who the hell are you? You new around here?"

"Ichinoses don't have the right to ask my name," he declared, drawing his sword.

In doing so, he left himself open. No—Guren realized he had only made it look as if he left himself open so that his opponent would underestimate him. Which meant he was strong.

And the idiotic attitude he had adopted when he confronted them in the hallway had just been an act to keep Shinya from accompanying them outside.

"I see you brought some friends along to help. You'll need it."

The boy smirked. "I can deal with the likes of you all on

my own."

His friends certainly seemed to believe it.

The boy, however, hadn't let his own power go to his head; he had laid down a trap as well. And even if Guren did prove to be too much for him, his friends were standing by to jump in.

Guren stared at them.

"..."

He could feel a faint desire spring to life within him.

How gratifying it would be to beat these cocky little twerps into a bloody pulp.

How much it would do for his self-esteem to cut loose and force them into submission.

To pummel their pathetic little leader, the one they believed in so fervently, until he was reduced to tears.

—*Forget tears, let's beat him to death. Then his friends will be the ones crying. "Stop, please," they'll say. "Oh please don't hurt him. We were wrong."*

"Quiet, demon."

—*But I represent your own desires.*

"And I can control you."

—*Are you sure? Then show me. Unsheathe me, and let's chop off this insolent brat's head.*

"Draw your weapon," said the boy.

Guren drew a shallow breath.

Mahiru continued.

—*Come on, hurry up. Let's show these fools who they're dealing with.*

Guren exhaled, ignoring her.

Then he breathed in a second time, and with a *hup*, he sprung forward.

Without drawing his sword.

—*Huh?*

Mahiru sounded surprised, but Guren ignored her as he closed the gap with his opponent.

The boy swung his sword at Guren. The strike was fast and keen, but Guren dodged it by a hair's breadth before following up with a right jab.

"Erk!"

The boy managed to dodge Guren's punch, but Guren used his momentum to grab one of the girls standing behind him by the neck.

"Wa—!" A shocked look appeared on the girl's face.

"Shit!"

"Watch out!" The boy's other friends shouted, all caught off guard.

Guren swung the girl about like a ragdoll, sending her

smashing into the boy's companions.

"Ack!"

Three of them went down. Meanwhile, Guren slipped a *fuda*—a paper charm inscribed with a spell—from his breast pocket. He slapped the *fuda* on the ground, positioning it to interfere with the part of the trap that had been laid there. Guren needed to place four *fuda,* in four different locations, to rewrite the spell pattern and take control of the trap.

One down.

"..."

Guren's senses were on high alert, growing sharper with each passing second.

He sensed the boy behind him, raising his sword above his head.

Guren stepped to the side without turning around.

The boy's blade sliced through open space and struck the ground.

"How?!" The boy blurted out in surprise, but Guren ignored him.

He threw another *fuda* at the trap. It took hold.

Two down.

Shinya was a natural at spellcraft, and Guren had a feeling that he would only have needed three *fuda* to short-circuit the trap. But Guren wasn't as talented at magic. He still needed four.

Guren spun around.

The boy seemed to finally realize how much more powerful Guren was, and he shouted, "Everyone draw your swords!"

But the words were barely out of the boy's mouth before Guren had kicked the girl beside him in the chest. That just left two of them standing: the boy himself and one other. They raised their swords with panicked expressions.

Guren ignored them, surreptitiously dropping another *fuda* onto the ground by his feet.

Three down.

"Hyaaaa!!"

The boy charged, blade first. He slashed downward, upward, in a wide lateral sweep.

Guren dodged. And dodged. And as he dodged the third stroke, he struck the boy's sword with the heel of his palm. The blade jerked to the side, half-severing the thigh of the boy's remaining friend.

"Agh!" He collapsed. The wound was deep. If not for the boy's cursed gear, it might've been fatal. Even with the curse, it would take some time to heal.

Now the boy alone remained.

"Dammiiiiiit!" he shouted, charging again.

Guren moved backward at precisely the same speed the boy advanced.

One step.

Two steps.

Three steps.

Four steps.

On the fifth step, even as he avoided the boy's blow, Guren stamped his foot, affixing the *fuda* he had hidden on the heel of his shoe to the ground.

That made four.

Guren now controlled the trap.

In that instant,

—Guren, that's not niiice.

But Guren continued to ignore Mahiru.

The boy fixed his eyes on Guren with a sneer. "You think you've won?"

Guren shrugged and returned the boy's stare. "Uh huh, sure do. Had enough?"

"You idiot. Look at you, standing there with that smug expression on your face. You've got no idea."

"That so?"

"Yeah. We laid a trap for you. And you were so busy showing off by not drawing your weapon that you never even noticed."

The boy's friends staggered back to their feet, ill-natured grins plastered across their faces. Even the boy with the thigh injury was smirking as he leaned against the girl beside him for support.

The leader pointed at the ground beneath Guren's feet. "We led you right into our trap!"

As he spoke, the outline of a spell barrier that had remained hidden up to that point began glowing in the dirt.

But of course, Guren had known about it from the start—

"You Ichinoses really are stupid, aren't you," laughed one of the girls. "Who cares if you're strong when you're dumb as an ox?"

"Bwahaha, how does it feel, knowing you fell into our trap? That's what you get for strutting around like a hero just because you got the power back on."

"Say you're sorry and maybe we'll forgive you. But you have to get down on your knees first. Get down in the dirt and say, 'I'm sorry, sir, for forgetting my place.' Go on. Do it!"

"Nng…" Guren groaned softly.

Mahiru appeared suddenly by his side. There she was, standing beside him like she had just danced down out of the sky.

—Didn't I tell you, Guren? How good it would feel?

Guren crossed his arms in consternation.

"Don't bother, you'll never think of a way out!" crowed the boy. "This barrier is impenetrable! Once you're in, the only way out is death. Unless, of course, I dispel it."

"…"

"Go ahead. Admit you were arrogant, and apologize."

"…"

"Get down on your knees and swear that you'll never get above your station again, never act like you can lead soldiers of the Order of the Imperial Demons."

The boy didn't seem to have the slightest inkling that Guren had already taken control of his trap.

"Come on, get on your knees."

"Yeah, do it. Get in the dirt!"

"What's wrong, don't you even know how to kneel?"

"Or are you so scared you can't move?"

—*Now then, how can we make this moment even more delicious?*

"*I think I missed my opportunity for the big reveal,*" replied Guren.

—*So you're planning to kneel?*

"*Not a chance.*"

—*Then let's have some fun. Let them know that you hijacked their trap in the most painful way possible.*

"*I bet you'd love that. I remember how you used to toy with me and Kureto, the way you'd tempt us, make fools of us.*"

—*Uh huh!*

"*I didn't think you'd cop to it just like that.*"

—*Haha. You don't like a girl who knows what she wants?*

"*…*"

—*Or is that just your type?*

"..."

—Hey, Guren.

"What?"

—We've got some nastier enemies watching us right now, in case you haven't noticed.

"Enemies?"

—Uh huh.

He looked at Mahiru. And saw that, for once, she seemed just a little bit tense.

Guren followed her gaze.

Five heads were poking out half-concealed from the entrance of the barracks.

It was Shinya, Norito, Mito, Shigure, and Sayuri. They were watching him surreptitiously.

They had probably realized what Guren was doing.

Which was why they hadn't stepped in to help.

Their eyes sparkled with anticipation, as they waited to see when Guren would tell the boy his trap had been hijacked.

—Don't you think we should give our audience what they want, Guren?

"*Be quiet...*" Guren groaned inwardly.

The boy and his friends, meanwhile, continued to taunt him.

"Come on, what the hell do you think you're doing!"

"We don't have all day!"

"Kneel! Kneel! Kneel!"

Guren could see Norito covering his mouth with his hands, stifling a laugh.

Guren stared off into the distance, his eyes losing focus.

"It's so peaceful," he murmured.

"Hanh?!" The boy seemed to have heard him, but Guren had lost interest.

He turned his attention toward his own friends, in the doorway.

"You guys aren't very nice," Guren called out.

"Look who's talking," Shinya yelled back.

The boy shouted angrily at Guren. "Stop trying to act like you're not about to piss your pants!"

Guren ignored him and began walking away.

"Wait, where are you going?! If you move, you'll be killed!"

But Guren kept ignoring him.

"If you trigger the trap, you'll die!"

Guren still ignored him.

"Fine, but don't blame me! It's your own fault for not listening!" called the boy, raising his arm into the air. He traced a cross in the air three times, the gesture to activate the magic circle.

The trap sprang to life. A net of bright light began to rise

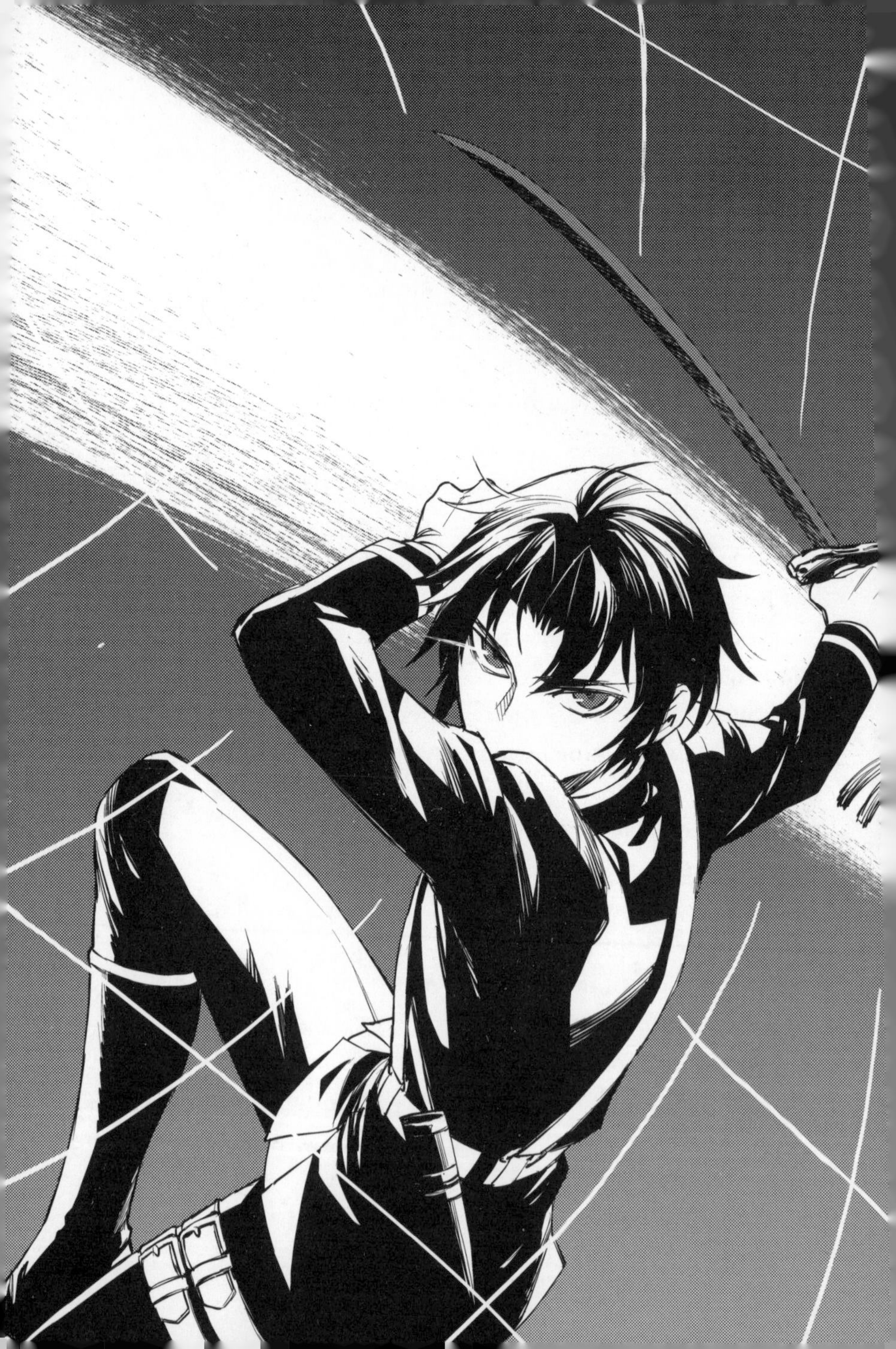

from the earth. Any normal person who touched those rays would be sliced to pieces.

Someone whose body had been strengthened by the demon's curse might not actually be dismembered, but the injuries would still be severe.

The net of light began to close in—not on Guren, however, but on the boy and his friends.

"Wh-What?!" the boy exclaimed.

"No way!" cried the girl.

"Somebody help!"

"No, nooo!"

Guren sighed. "What a fucking pain in the ass." He finally unsheathed his sword for the first time and dashed forward.

As the rays of light began to close in on the boy and his friends, Guren struck, slicing through the net and saving them.

A look of surprise crossed the boy's face. "Th… Th… Thank y—" he began, but before he could finish Guren raised his fist, the one holding his sword, and punched him in the face.

"Ngh!" The boy collapsed to his knees.

"Thank you?" Guren shouted. "Don't you get it yet, you little shit? You just nearly got your friends killed, all over some petty personal vendetta!"

The boy looked up, pressing a hand to his face. His friends stared at Guren with fear in their eyes.

"Or did someone order you to do this? One of your superior officers? Go pick on the Ichinose trash, was that it?!"

The boy was speechless, but Guren didn't wait for a response. "I don't care if it *was* an order, that still doesn't excuse what you did. You underestimated me, and put your teammates' lives in danger! You were too busy calling me names to realize the situation you were in!"

"I..."

"You should have used your trap right away. They put their lives in your hands, and you owed it to them to make sure you were absolutely prepared before attacking me. What would you have done if I had drawn my weapon from the start? If I had cut that girl's head off with my first strike?! Who would have been responsible for that?!" shouted Guren, pointing at the girl.

—*Oh, so that's why you left me in my sheath? You wanted to give a speech?*

Guren ignored Mahiru and went on. "No matter how much reconnaissance you do, how well you plan, you'll still lose people. That's what happens on a battlefield. But did you care? What was the point of all this? Look at your team, they believe in you. Do you realize what you did? Coming after me unprepared, all for a personal vendetta? Does that kind of behavior deserve their trust?! Well? Answer me!"

"I... I..."

"When your friends die, there's no bringing them back!" Guren shouted.

It was true.

And if you wanted to overturn that truth, you had to be prepared to pay an unthinkable price.

"I'm... I'm sorry," the boy apologized.

But Guren wasn't interested in an apology.

—*You just wanted to prove you were right to make yourself feel better, didn't you?*

Guren ignored her.

—*Or maybe it's just self-flagellation. Does it make it easier for you, to punish yourself for failing to protect your friends?*

"Shut up. Go away."

—*Oh, but it wasn't your fault, Guren... Is that what you want to hear?*

"I told you to go away."

And she finally did.

Guren returned his sword to its sheath.

"Mis-ter Cool!" shouted Shinya and the others as they approached. They were clearly making fun of him.

"What are you doing out here? You should be in bed already!" Guren said to his friends—the friends he had failed to protect.

Guren was just like the boy, in the end. His friends trusted him. They risked their lives for him. But Guren was never strong enough, never well enough prepared.

"I... I'm sorry..." came a voice from behind Guren.

The boy's voice.

The boy's friends all responded immediately.

"You don't need to apologize, Kuro. It's our fault for not being strong enough."

"M-My parents always taught me that the Ichinoses were just worthless mongrels, too... This was just as much my fault," they insisted.

The boy got back to his feet. He looked up at Guren. "No, I fuc—this was my mistake. I should have realized how strong you were, as the leader of the Ichinose Clan. Please, leave them out of it. If anyone deserves to be punished for this..."

Guren looked at the boy. "You still don't get it, do you? What if you *had* won? What then? You think this is any time for personal squabbles?"

"I..."

"What's your name?"

"..."

"Your name."

"It's Kuro... Kuro Kuki."

Now it was all starting to make sense.

The Kuki Clan, like the Goshis and Jujos, was one of the great houses that had supported the Hiragi Clan since time immemorial. There were nine such clans:

Nii, Sangu, Shijin, Goshi, Rikudo, Shichikai, Hakke, Kuki, and Jujo.

But two of those clans, the Niis and the Kukis, had joined

the Brotherhood of a Thousand Nights and rebelled against the Hiragis right before the world had come to an end.

Actually, Guren was only certain about the Nii Clan. The head of the Nii Clan had led an army against Kureto, and the clan had been wiped out as a result.

But Guren had heard that much of the Kuki Clan had also been purged.

"What happened to the rest of your clan?"

Kuro's face contorted in pain. "They're all dead."

"Why are you still alive?"

"I… I was a bastard, a lovechild. The Hiragis had taken me as a hostage…"

That explained why he was still alive. They had let him live because there was proof positive that he hadn't been involved in his clan's betrayal.

And Kuro must have attacked Guren in an attempt to wash away the stain on his family's name.

"So you thought you could prove yourself by beating me?"

"…"

It seemed Guren had hit the nail on the head. It was just the kind of superficial thinking you'd expect from a child, only looking out for number one.

But the boy shook his head, a tortured expression on his face. "B-Because of my name, my team is always getting overlooked. Even though…even though we've already achieved so much…"

The boy's friends all gathered around and patted him on the shoulder.

He was lucky to have such good friends. He was probably a

decent leader most of the time.

Guren sympathized.

After all, he had been branded as a traitor his entire life.

It had probably gotten under the boy's skin that Guren, who was supposedly just a traitorous Ichinose mongrel, was suddenly making such a name for himself.

"Now that we've fought, though, I finally get it," Kuro said. "Just how strong you are. Strong enough to shake off the label of a traitor."

"..."

"If only I was as strong as you—"

Guren cut him off. "How old are you?"

"Fourteen."

"I'll be seventeen soon. By the time you're seventeen, you'll probably be stronger than I am now."

"No way... You're on a whole different level..."

"It doesn't matter how strong the other guy is," Guren shot back, looking Kuro straight in the eye. "You can always catch up if you really try. Or would you rather tell your friends they should give up?"

"Oh." The boy opened his mouth, at a loss for words. A moment later he clenched his jaw and nodded, as if he had suddenly seen things in a different light. "You're right, we've got work to do."

"That's better," said Guren, swatting him lightly on the top of the head.

Then he sighed, and turned around to face his friends. They were all staring at him, pleased as punch.

Guren glared back at them. "What are you looking at?"

"I think you just made a few more fans," answered Shinya. Guren ignored him.

"I-I fast-forwarded the tape," said Mito. "You lied to us!"

"You mean you actually watched it? I had no idea you were such a pervert."

"WHAT did you just call me?!" Mito's face flushed bright red and she swung at Guren full force, but Guren caught her fist lightly in one hand.

Behind them, Kuro and his friends watched excitedly.

"Did you see how fast he blocked that?"

"Isn't that Mito, from the Jujo Clan? I can't believe it!"

"Lieutenant Guren is amazing…"

"Careful you don't get addicted to all the praise," Norito smirked, but Guren ignored him as well.

Mito, Sayuri, and Shigure, meanwhile, kept harping on about the video.

"What were you thinking, showing us something like that?!"

"I-Is that the sort of thing you'd like to do, Master Guren? Because i-i-if it is, I'm ready any time to—"

"Sayuri! Who said you could have Master Guren all to yourself?"

Guren ignored them all and headed back into the barracks.

He could hear Kuro and his friends laughing as he walked away.

And even though it was long past bedtime, the children inside were still laughing and squealing as well.

"Even with everything that's happened," said Shinya, coming up beside Guren, "having all these kids around really gives you hope for the future, doesn't it?"

Guren looked over at Shinya. *"So despite everything, are you glad you survived?"* was what he wanted to ask, but he bit his tongue. If Guren asked something like that, Shinya would catch on in no time.

So Guren worded it a different way.

"You're right. Having all these kids around makes life still seem worthwhile."

"Huh. I never took you for the doting father type, Guren."

"A doting father with a sordid past in porn."

"Hahaha."

Things really had grown peaceful. It was like none of the bad stuff, the scary stuff, had ever happened.

Things were just ordinary.

Sure, the world may have ended, but everyday life went on. Todays turned into tomorrows.

Guren was finally starting to feel like he could breathe again.

Peace.

Everyday, ordinary peace.

They arrived in front of Guren's room.

It was time to get some sleep. They had to be on duty early again tomorrow.

"You going to bed?" asked Shinya.

Guren nodded. "Yeah. There was something really peaceful about today. I'm looking forward to some good dreams for once."

"Nothing like a nice, peaceful dream."

"Yeah."

"Or a dirty one."

"Now you're talking."

"Yeah. Anyway, goodnight."

"'Night." Guren nodded and opened the door. It was a simple room, with just a desk and a bed.

It was dark inside. But on the bed lay something to shatter all those dreams of peace and make the everyday suddenly seem farther away than ever.

"..."

Guren slammed the door shut again in front of him.

Norito happened to be passing by at that exact moment. "Something wrong?"

"What? No..."

"Come on, what is it?"

"I was just thinking I should go to the bathroom before I go to bed."

"Oh. Well, I'm gonna turn in too," Norito replied before walking away.

"I expect an explanation tomorrow, Guren!" called out Mito as she passed by.

"Goodnight, Master Guren."

"Sleep well," said Sayuri and Shigure as they headed down the hallway.

Guren nodded at each of them, and then headed toward the bathroom. He did his business and washed his hands, taking his time at the sink, getting his hands extra clean—anything to delay going back to his room.

Maybe I was just imagining things, he thought to himself as the water poured over his soapy hands.

Because if what he saw was real, he wouldn't be getting any sleep tonight. His days of peace and quiet had just come to a screeching halt.

Guren left the bathroom.

He walked down the hall, and stood before his bedroom door once again.

The barracks was silent. The children must have finally run out of steam.

Guren stared at the door. He opened it and stepped inside. The room was still dark.

"..."

A man with silver hair lay sprawled across the bed in the middle of the dark room.

A vampire noble.

Ferid Bathory.

His eyes were closed. Could he be asleep?

A girl lay by his side.

Guren focused his senses on the girl. Was she breathing?

Was her heart beating?

Ferid's eyes opened a crack. "I didn't kill her. I drained her almost to the brink, but I knew you'd be angry if I killed her."

"What the hell are you doing here?" demanded Guren, turning on the light. The darkness put him at a disadvantage. Vampires had perfect nightvision.

Of course, Ferid was so powerful that he would have no

problem killing Guren if he wanted to, regardless.

Ferid sat up and turned toward the door. His bewitching red eyes were fixated on Guren as he spoke. "First of all, don't you think you should thank me? 'Thank you sir, for saving me the last time we met.'"

"..."

"If it wasn't for me, you'd already be dead. That vampire patrol would've killed you. Do you have any idea what I went through for your sake? I took on a vampire of higher rank. But I'm getting ahead of myself. Perhaps you'd like to hear about what that really entails?"

"No thanks."

"I think you would."

"I said I'm good."

"Here I go then. You see, I'm of the seventh rank. The woman I fought was of the sixth. In the hierarchy of high-ranked progenitors, a single step represents an incredible jump in power. A monster of a completely different order. In other words, I faced down impossible odds for you."

Guren stepped inside the room and closed the door.

He couldn't let anyone find out about this. After all, Ferid had been there when Guren brought Shinya and the others back to life.

"And it wasn't just her, she had an entire unit at her back," added Ferid, breezily. "Let's see, there were... How many were there? I don't know how many there were, but it was definitely a lot. Naturally, for a noble such as myself, ordinary vampires like that are just the ragtag and bobtail, so it hardly matters how many of them there were. But still, I put in quite an effort."

Ferid stared at Guren with a hangdog expression, like he was waiting for Guren to pat him on the head and tell him what a good job he had done.

"So you want me to...congratulate you?" asked Guren.

"Naturally."

"Thank...you for—"

"No no no, that's not it at all."

"Huh?"

"Take a look at my face. You've got to learn to read between the lines. I don't care about gratitude anymore. I'm over it. What I want is your adulation."

"For...fighting a vampire of a higher rank?"

"Not that."

"For fighting so many vampires all at once?"

"Oh come on, not that either. It's something even bigger. Think!"

"..."

Guren tried, but he drew a blank. What in the world was Ferid referring to?

"I give up," Guren eventually admitted.

"Ragtag and bobtail," said Ferid, looking pleased.

"What about it?"

"Do you know what it means?"

"What it means? Like, the definition?"

"Yes."

"A...group of worthless people?"

"Bingo! But tell me, do you all use that expression often?"

Guren gave it some thought. Had he ever used the phrase in his life?

Come to think of it, he was pretty sure he hadn't. Guren shook his head. "I don't think so, no."

At this, Ferid leapt up from the bed in excitement. "You see? I'm not even human, but I knew the expression and used it in a sentence. I'm probably the first person to use it since the world was destroyed. If that's not praiseworthy, then what is? I'm saving human language, practically single-handed. Though the truth is, I saw the phrase in a book I was reading yesterday in my spare time, and I had to look it up in the dictionary."

This just kept getting weirder. What was Ferid's point?

He was going on and on about some expression he had just learned.

While all the time an eight-year-old girl lay on the bed behind him.

Ferid said he hadn't killed her, but Guren couldn't hear her breathing.

Nor could he hear her heartbeat.

"The thing is, when I went to the library, all the bookcases had fallen over, and it took me positively forever to find a dictionary."

"You said you didn't kill her."

"Plus, it's something of an outdated expression. I could find 'ragtag,' but no 'bobtail.' And when I finally did find 'bobtail,' it didn't have anything to do with people! It took three hours before I finally found a dictionary old enough to—"

"Hey, you said—"

Ferid cut him off abruptly, a smile still plastered across his face. "So what?"

"..."

"I made things easier for you this way. You wouldn't want anyone to see us talking, would you? If they did, you'd have been forced to kill them. To murder this poor, innocent little girl, as the tears streamed down your face. Aren't you glad that I prevented that?"

"I would never do something like that."

"Really? You wouldn't? Then why did you bring your friends back to life? You're not making any sense. After killing so many people, you're going to pretend to be a good boy now?"

"..."

"You would have killed her. We both know it. Because if anyone were to see us, your precious resurrected friends might vanish forever."

"I wouldn't."

"Oh but you would."

"I w—"

An expression of absolute delight suddenly crossed Ferid's face. He raised his hand high into the air and dove backward onto the bed, his fist coming down on the girl's chest.

Thud.

And a split second later:

"Hurrrk," the girl sucked in air.

Her eyes opened.

And turned toward Guren.

"Dammit." Guren quickly covered his face with one hand

and drew his sword with the other, turning it around and smacking the girl on the back of the neck with the flat of the blade. She lost consciousness once more.

"By the way," said Ferid, sitting on the bed and grinning at Guren, "while I was draining her blood, I told this girl that the world had been destroyed because you resurrected Shinya Hiragi and your other friends. Are you sure you don't want to kill her?"

Guren glared at Ferid.

Ferid smiled again. "Just kidding. She doesn't know anything, she isn't even from around here. I brought her along as my meat canteen."

"Why are you doing this?"

"Because I knew your reaction would be priceless."

"But what's the point?"

"Point? Does anything in this world really have a point anymore?"

"..."

Guren didn't know how to answer.

Was there really meaning left in this world?

In their lives?

Was there any reason not to just throw in the towel?

"I'm the one asking you," Guren said to Ferid, the ancient vampire sitting there before him. "Why do all this, if you think it's meaningless? Why go on living at all?"

"Hmm."

"If life is so pointless, then why not just die already?"

Ferid grinned. "It's true, I have lived far too long. As vam-

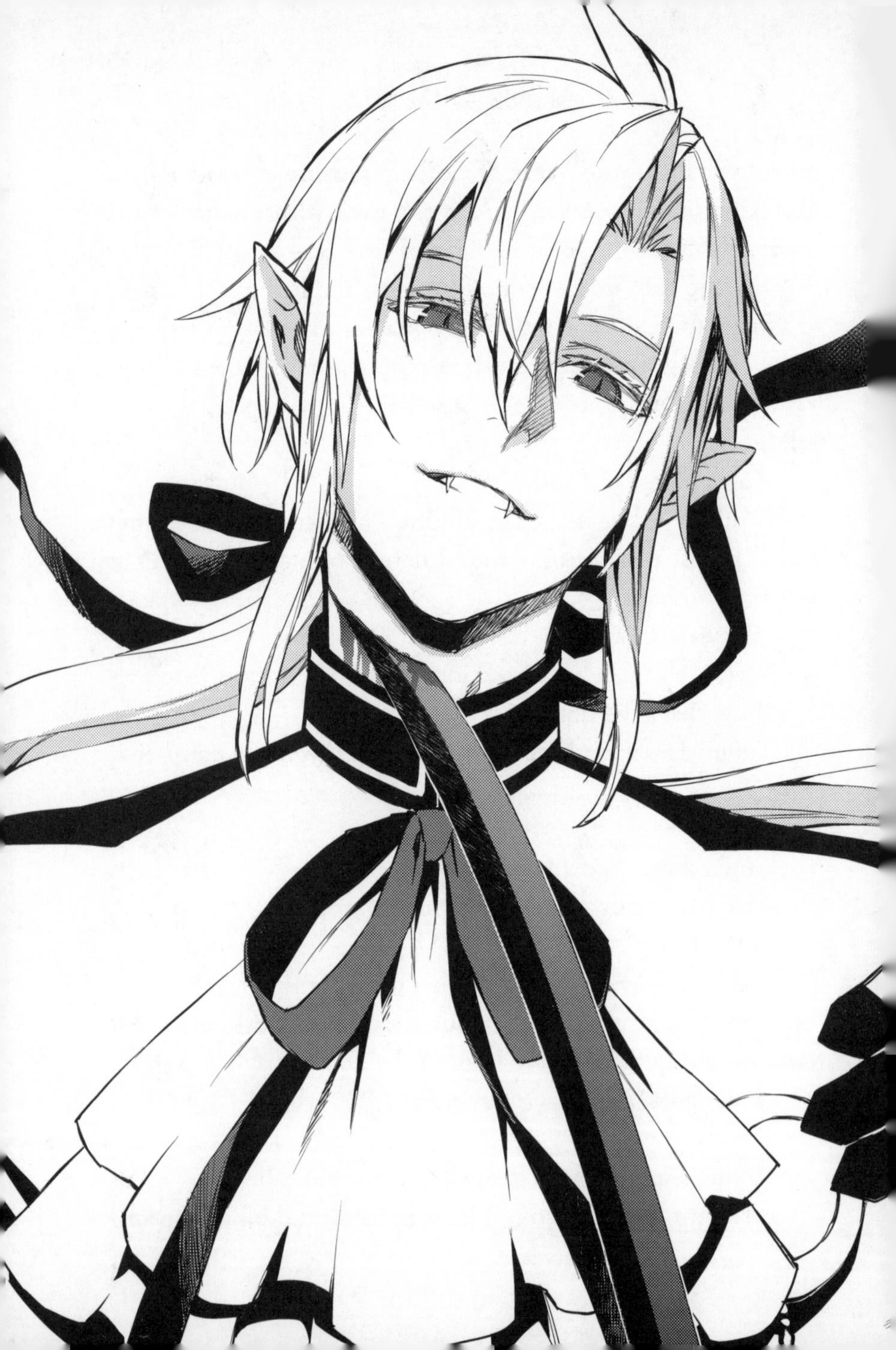

pires, the more we age, the more we lose the ability to feel anything at all. Only the desire for blood remains. It's so tedious. We don't even sleep. Every day is so long, and yet so short, and yet—none of it matters, so it feels endless. Five years can pass in the blink of an eye, and you look around and realize nothing has changed. Can you imagine?"

"So why don't you just die already?"

"Haha, why don't you kill me?" Ferid replied, exposing his pale, white neck.

Leaning in, toward Guren's sword.

"You want me to kill you?"

"You said I should die, didn't you? So put your money where your mouth is."

What kind of a game was Ferid playing?

Did life have meaning or not?

Guren raised his sword and levelled it at Ferid. He took a step closer. The tip of the blade touched Ferid's throat.

Ferid didn't move. "Hurry up," he said, his eyes sparkling with delight.

Guren slid the blade into Ferid's neck.

The blade punctured the vampire's skin easily, sinking into the side of his neck and coming out the back.

"Ah, is today the day I finally die?" Ferid wondered aloud, his expression as carefree as ever.

This was Guren's chance.

Unlike a normal weapon, cursed gear could affect a vampire's body, could even destroy it.

If he wanted to kill Ferid, all he had to do was unleash the sword's power and let its magic flow.

Ferid closed one eye, almost as if he was winking. "Do it," he said with a grin.

"But why?" Guren asked. "What's the point of it all?"

"How many times do I have to tell you? There is no point."

" . . ."

"Nothing has meaning, nothing at all. Even if I die here today, so what? What does it matter?"

"Then why are you here?"

At this Ferid reached out to Guren and touched his cheek. "You bear his scent."

"Scent?"

"Yes."

"Whose?"

"My father's. Is it your own smell? Or is it just on you? You've met Rígr Stafford, haven't you?" asked Ferid.

Rígr Stafford. The second-rank progenitor.

Wasn't that Saito's real name?

Ferid had called Saito his father, but what was that supposed to mean? Was he his biological father, or did Ferid mean something else?

Saito had said that he inserted his own tissue into the Ichinose bloodline hundreds of years ago. Did Ferid know about that?

Guren glared at the vampire. "Your father? What's that supposed to mean? What's your connection to Saito?"

"I thought you were going to kill me?"

"Just answer the question."

"I already have. Rígr Stafford is the one who turned me into a vampire. As a rule, vampires hate their parents. It's they who cursed us with these deathless bodies, after all. See for yourself." Ferid grabbed the blade of Guren's sword where it was embedded in his neck and worked it further in. "It's bad enough that we are deathless, but we are made insensate as well, unable even to fear death."

"So...what? You want revenge?"

But Ferid just rolled his eyes toward the ceiling. "Revenge? I wonder. Even that thought leaves me cold."

"Then what is it you want?"

"Can't you guess?"

"How should I know?"

"Well, I know. I know exactly what I want."

"I would hope so."

"Do you want to know what it is?"

"No."

"Shall I tell you?"

"I don't want to know."

But Ferid ignored him. "This! This is what I want!"

The vampire opened his mouth wide and, heedless of the blade skewering his own neck, clamped his jaws around Guren's throat.

"Grk!"

Ferid began to drink.

Guren, meanwhile, put all his strength into the hand gripping his sword. All he had to do was let the magic flow, and Ferid would be no more. The curse would worm its way into

Ferid's body and tear his head from his shoulders.

He could kill Ferid at any moment.

"But you won't, will you," Ferid exulted. "I'm your only real friend, the only one who watched the world crumble by your side. And besides, Rígr Stafford…or should I say Saito, is manipulating you, isn't he? Something else we have in common. So you can't kill me. You need the information I have."

"…"

"Unless, of course, I'm wrong. But if today is the day I die, then so be it. Well, is it? Is today the day?"

"…"

Ferid continued to drink.

Gulp after gulp.

Guren hated how good it felt to be drained of his blood this way.

"Dammit…" he groaned.

Guren could tell that Ferid was holding back this time. He had drunk much more greedily in the elevator.

But today he was taking his time.

"Aren't you going to kill me?" Ferid asked again.

"Aren't *you* going to kill *me*?" Guren replied.

"Of course not. We made a pact, didn't we? I'm to be your guide through this ruined world. Remember how you begged me? *Please, O my lord and master.*"

Guren made to release the sword's power,

"Oopsie-daisy!" but Ferid hurriedly retreated a few steps.

"I guess you didn't want to die after all," observed Guren, staring at Ferid.

The vampire shrugged. "I honestly wouldn't mind, but you have to be in earnest... A half-hearted attempt like that would've been very painful, but it wouldn't have killed me."

The hole in Ferid's throat closed before Guren's very eyes. Ferid rubbed the spot, making sure it had healed. "I can taste it. You have—"

"—Saito's blood running in my veins," Guren finished.

"You knew, then. Who told you? Was it the man himself?"

"..."

"When? When did he contact you?"

"You seem very interested all of a sudden."

"I haven't seen him in so long, can you blame me? I'm like little Marco in *3000 Leagues in Search of Mother*, you see, wandering the earth in search of my long-lost parents. So I was right, then. He is in Japan. I guess it was worth coming here after all."

Ferid's face suddenly grew serious. He appeared to be pondering something. And. As he was finally asking, "What did he want from you," Mahiru appeared out of nowhere behind him.

She looked at Guren and put a finger lightly to her lips.

Hush.

Mahiru was connected to Saito.

She was part of his plan.

Or was Saito part of hers?

Guren wasn't sure.

Mahiru was a genius. She was terrifyingly smart, well beyond Guren's reckoning.

The same probably held true for Saito. Apparently he even

had this mad vampire on a string.

Ferid suddenly narrowed his eyes.

He swung around sharply. "What's this? There seems to be something here."

Mahiru looked down her nose at Ferid, just a hint of surprise registering on her face.

"I can't see it, but I sense a presence. And whatever it is, I don't like it."

At this, Mahiru spoke.

—*Kill him, Guren. He's going to interfere with our plans.*

So Ferid was capable of causing trouble for Mahiru? Or rather, for Mahiru and Saito?

Guren wasn't sure what those two were planning, but Mahiru had suddenly decided that this vampire was in their way.

"Who's here?" asked Ferid. "Can you see?"

—*Kill him, Guren. Do it now! Quickly!*

The power in Guren's sword began to swirl out of control.

Dark magic enveloped his arm.

"Seriously?" Ferid scoffed, glancing at Guren's arm. "You don't honestly plan to fight me, do you?"

Guren didn't know what to do.

Should he listen to Mahiru?

Or should he make a deal with this mad vampire, to fill in some of the missing pieces of the puz—

Mahiru interrupted his thoughts. She seemed to realize what he was thinking.

—Obviously I'm the one you should trust. Don't try to resist me. Let your power run wild, and—

The sword suddenly flew from Guren's hand, and began spinning in the air of its own accord.

—Kill him!

The sword's blade was pointed at Ferid. Guren grabbed the hilt in a desperate attempt to stop it.

"Run, Ferid Bathory," he said through gritted teeth.

"Eh?"

"Mahiru is trying to kill you."

"Mahiru? The Hiragi girl? Is she here now?"

"She's inside me."

"Oho, so Mahiru's will lives on. I wonder if she's just a delusion you've cooked up, or if she's something more."

Guren began to lose control, the rampaging demonic power drawing him closer and closer to the edge.

Dark magic flowed from the sword into Guren's body, and he was powerless to stop it.

His right arm was now jet black.

"Stop it, Mahiru."

Ferid laughed. "Even if Mahiru is here, why would she want to kill me? If anything, I'm on your side, Guren Ichinose. We share a common enemy: Saito. Poor Guren, I think the little bitch has betrayed you, and bedded down with hi—"

The sword suddenly moved again, flickering a hair's breadth from Ferid's neck.

"Yikes, scary." Ferid retreated toward the bed, lightly patting his neck. "But far too slow. You'll never take my head like that. You'll have to do better if you want to frighten me, Mahiru, my dear."

But it was becoming harder and harder for Guren to hear Ferid's voice.

His mind was drowning in inky blackness, consumed with a single dark word: kill.

Kill kill kill
Kill kill kill kill kill kill

Kill kill kill everything in your path—
"Mahiru, stop."

—*It's alright, Guren, relax. Just go to sleep. It'll all be over by the time you wake up. I'll take care of everything.*

"You're trying to possess me."

—*No, Guren. I am you. And you are me.*

"You're…"

—Sleep. Just leave it all to me,

"I'll take care of everything," said the young man standing before him.

But there was a feminine tone to his voice now. The dark magic had spread across his entire body. It looked as if he had been completely taken over by his demon.

"Interesting," murmured Ferid Bathory, trying to size up what exactly he was seeing. "Has little Mahiru come out to play?"

"Try to show a little more respect when you speak to me," the demon replied.

"How about Miss Mahiru, then."

"I'm going to kill you."

"Hahaha. And how do you plan to do that? You're not strong enough. But I think you already know that."

"…"

"Let's have a little chat instead. Tell me, have you been Rígr Stafford's dog all along?"

Guren grinned. It was a strangely bewitching smile, clearly belonging to someone else. "You're one to talk. You've got serious daddy issues, Ferid Bathory. Can't seem to get your father off your mind, can you?"

"Finally, someone who understands me! I was shat out of my father's asshole, you see. Papa, papa, where are you papa! It's dark in here, and I'm ever so scared—"

Guren attacked suddenly, before Ferid could finish his

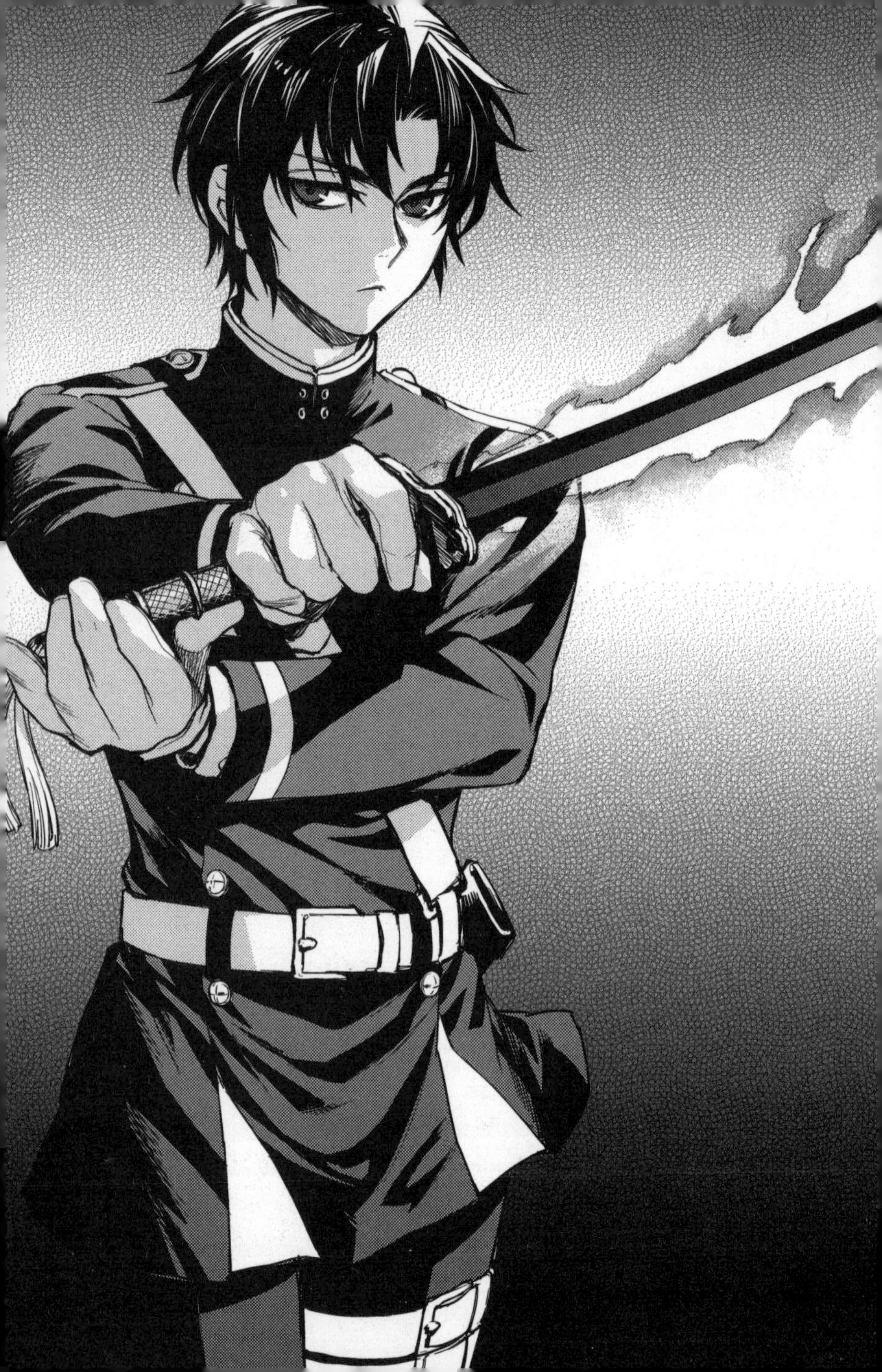

sentence.

He swung his sword faster than any human being possibly could. The blade travelled in a straight line, aimed unerringly at Ferid's neck. However,

"I told you, you're too slow."

Ferid lunged forward twice as fast, burying his fist in his opponent's face. Ferid felt the skull collapse beneath his punch. Guren's body—whether inhabited by Guren himself or by Mahiru, he didn't know—began to crumple to the ground, knees buckling, and only managed to stay upright by planting the sword in the floor.

"How many times do I have to tell you, you'll never beat me like that," Ferid said as he watched Guren's crushed skull heal almost instantaneously. "So why come out now, Mahiru Hiragi?"

Guren lifted his head and looked at Ferid. "To kill you."

"On whose orders?"

"Ahaha."

"It doesn't matter. You're not capable of killing me."

"Are you sure about that?"

"If you think you can do it, go ahead and try."

"You forget, Ferid Bathory, this is Shibuya," said Guren, smiling up at him. "The headquarters of the most vicious magical syndicate in existence. You're in the lion's den."

"And? Are you planning to alert everyone to my presence so you can attack me all at once? If you do that, they'll all find out who you and Guren brought back from the dead. And then Shinya Hiragi and all your other little friends will—"

But Guren—or rather, Mahiru Hiragi—interrupted him

with a laugh. "Those are Guren's pathetic attachments, they've got nothing to do with me."

Guren's sword whistled through the air.

It struck the bed, slicing both the bed itself and the little girl lying on it in two. It cleaved through the wall behind the bed as well, and the wall behind that, and the one behind that, on and on in a train of destruction, surely killing dozens more.

This girl was insane. She had just ravaged the building in spectacular fashion, while slaughtering scores of her supposed friends in the process.

And then,

"VAMPIIIIIRE! A VAMPIRE NOBLE HAS PENETRATED THE BARRACKS!"

An alarm sounded immediately.

Ferid sensed murderous intent welling up on all sides.

Dozens, hundreds, thousands of soldiers equipped with cursed gear flooding towards him.

"…"

Ferid narrowed his eyes.

He focused, honing his perception. He could pinpoint every foe, read their strengths, their movements, their next moves.

"Oh dear, and you looked so sure of yourself a moment ago," clucked Guren. "I guess today is the day after all. Do you hear me, Ferid Bathory? Today is your final day. Today is the day you die."

Perhaps she was right at that.

If so, then so be it, thought Ferid.

He had no illusions. After all those centuries, he was acutely aware that life had no meaning. There was virtually nothing and no one he would miss.

Nevertheless, he calculated.

How many seconds until the enemy arrived? How powerful was each foe?

And he considered.

How like a game this was.

How much of it might be going just as Rígr Stafford had imagined. If Mahiru really wanted to kill him, she could have done so earlier, when Guren's sword was buried in his neck. But she hadn't.

Hadn't, or hadn't been able to? Was it Mahiru who was calling the shots? Or was it Ferid's father?

Could he let the humans find out he was in league with Guren Ichinose, or was that better kept secret?

Which was furthest from Rígr Stafford's designs? The more Ferid thought, the more tangled the web became. If he hadn't known better, he would have almost said he was beginning to enjoy this game.

"No, today won't be the day, I think," he said with a grin. He could already hear voices coming up behind him. His foes seemed strong, and they were almost upon him.

"Raimeiki, roar!"

"Byakkomaru, go!"

Ferid cackled with delight. For the first time in ages he called on his full strength, and felt it fill his body. "Looks like I'll have to find another day to die."

It's out!

Seraph of the End – Guren Ichinose: Resurrection at Nineteen.

Pheeewwwwww, they announced the publication date before I had finished, and I really thought I was done for this time around, but I pulled some all-nighters and managed it in the end.

Usually I use the afterword to write about what's been going on lately, like so.

But I've been working so hard on finishing the manuscript that there's nothing much worth writing about. And every time I'm staring down the deadline for a novel, I end up having to work around the clock, so I wind up a total mess and catch a cold as soon as everything's submitted.

The truth is that as soon as I finish a manuscript I get all buzzed and wind up going to see a movie or something, even though I've barely been getting any sleep, and that's why I end up catching a cold. But this time I didn't even go to see a movie and I caught a cold anyway! It must be because it's gotten so chilly out.

Guren Ichinose: Resurrection at Nineteen

By the way, Guren and his friends don't catch colds. They're already infected with the demon's curse, so other viruses and bacteria can't take hold. Their bodies just return to their ideal state. Seems kind of vampire-ish to me.

But even after you're infected by a demon, you still grow older.

With vampirism, time stops, and you no longer age.

Much of this series is concerned with the question of whether we can still be human when things like that are true.

Life has no meaning.

Nor does death.

So why go on living?

I think a lot about such things while I'm writing.

And as I've been going over all this stuff in my head—the meaning of life, humans, demons, vampires—I've gotten to write about what happens after the end of the world in *Jump SQ*; what happens before the end of the world in *Monthly Shonen Magazine*; and the immediate aftermath in these novels.

We're steadily getting closer to the heart of the story.

Writing these novels has been very difficult because they get into the thought processes and internal lives of key characters, but I'm giving it my best. Thanks as always, and I hope you'll keep reading!

Takaya Kagami

TAKAYA KAGAMI

The closer we get to the heart of the story, the more I study the structure of various religions. Guren and his friends are only sixteen, but they spend so much time pondering the meaning of life that I figure I need to power myself up in that regard as well.

YO ASAMI (Illustrator)

I'm a manga artist and illustrator.

I'm currently doing the art for the manga version of *Seraph of the End – Guren Ichinose: Catastrophe at Sixteen*, which is being serialized in Monthly Shonen.

The collected editions are on sale too, so please check them out.

6-29-22
NEVER
0